I0721307

Sion

The Boy Who Barely Speaks

NASH DE LOS SANTOS

Copyright © 2025 Nash de los Santos

Printed in the United Kingdom.

Cover design by: Nash Delos Santos

Interior design by: Noble Legacy Publishing

ISBN: 978-1-911761-34-1

Dedication

To **Riza,**
who carries love like light, even through the hardest nights.

And to **Shann,**
whose quiet strength and beautiful mind inspired every
page of this story. You are the whisper the world needed to
hear.

With all my heart— this book is for you.

Also By The Author

1. When It Hurts To Believe

2. SION :2

THE WHISPERING CHRONICLES

PROLOGUE

Some children arrive with noise— kicking, wailing, full of
the world's wanting.
But not him.

Sion was born in silence.

Not the kind that frightens a room or sends nurses reaching
for charts.
His was the kind that felt... purposeful.
Like the world had taken a breath and paused, just for him.

He didn't cry much.
Didn't fuss the way others did.
He looked around, as if listening to something the rest of us
couldn't hear.

Even before he could hold a pencil, he noticed things most
people missed.
He'd fix his eyes on corners of rooms, on strangers passing
by, on skies just before rain.

And sometimes, he would whisper.
Not loud enough for full sentences, just fragments.
Words that arrived early… or too late.
Words that made no sense until they did.

He didn't fit in the places he was expected to.
Not at school.
Not at parties.
Not in loud church halls where other children ran circles
while he sat by the window,
watching leaves move without wind.

There were fears, of course.
From teachers.
From neighbours.
Even from us, his family.
But deeper than fearwas a quiet ache to understand him.
To follow him into whatever world he walked in when ours
became too sharp.

This story is not just about a boy who barely speak.
It's about what happens when the world stops long enough
to listen anyway.
It's about silence that heals.
Pain that moves.
And love that lingers
even when you cannot name it.

So begin here, with the boy who whispered.
And the world that never hears.

Contents

CHAPTER 1

The Boy Who Whispers

Sion lived in a small house on the edge of Circle Wood. Tucked away in a quiet cul-de-sac, the house was modest with two bedrooms, an odd little storage room, and a tiny room with a large window that looked out over a hidden brook. Most days, that fourth room was empty, gathering dust. But sometimes, when he needed it, Sion would go in there, sit by the window, and just watch.

His name was pronounced "Shawn."

Not "See-on," the way strangers often guessed when reading it aloud. Just Sion, quiet, soft, like a breath that barely made it out.

His father named him. It was a strange day. A hard one. His mother had gone in for an emergency caesarean after the doctors couldn't find a heartbeat. Sion wasn't moving. No flutter. No kick. For a long hour, they prepared for the worst.

His father waited outside the theatre with fingers clenched into each other, praying, pacing, whispering things he didn't even believe he believed. There were visitors in the family room, friends who'd come early, from Llandough, bringing comfort food and light chatter to fill the silence. One held a big bucket of KFC, his mother's favourite. She never ate much when nervous, but she always smiled at the smell.

Then came the cry.

Not loud. Just enough.

A nurse peeked her head out, smiled, and nodded. *"He's here."*

His father didn't speak. He walked over to the glass where they cleaned the newborn, staring through the reflections. The baby was still. So still. But his chest lifted, slow and steady. And when his eyes opened, just for a moment, they seemed… aware. *"Sion,"* his father whispered. It wasn't a name they'd discussed. It just came. Like something remembered from a dream.

Later, he'd explain it meant a high place. A place of refuge. Somewhere people ran to when the world became too much. A place where prayers went. *"He's not loud,"* the father said. *"But he's here. That's more than enough."* And so the name stayed. Like a promise. Or a prayer that got answered, softly.

In autumn, when the trees let go of their leaves, the brook revealed itself, just barely. A soft shimmer beneath bare branches. The water whispered across smooth stones, shy and secretive, like it didn't want to be found. Birds hopped along the branches and sang their morning songs. Sion liked it best when no one else was awake.

Sion was born in the UK, though his parents had come from the Philippines. They carried their accents with them like heavy suitcases, never fully unpacked, always part of the room. His mother would often say, *"He's just quiet, anak. Like your lolo."* His father, less patient, sometimes muttered things under his breath, words that weren't meant to be cruel but landed that way all the same.

He didn't speak. Or rather, he did, but only in whispers. Barely there. Like the brook. Like the wind. His parents had learned not to ask him to repeat himself. If they caught the words the first time, good. If not, it wasn't coming again.

Sion only ate rice, Spam and hot chocolate. Every day. Breakfast. Lunch. Dinner. The rice had to be jasmine, nothing else. If it wasn't, and if it wasn't warm and in his usual white bowl, he wouldn't even go near it. His mother tried once to add a fried chicken. He stared at it for ten minutes, unmoving, then walked away. After that, they stopped trying.

His father tried cooking different recipes just so he could have a taste of everything. He once roasted a whole chicken and called it "sitting chicken," because it sat upright in the big dish like it had somewhere to be. He tried "rellenong manok", painstakingly removing the bones and stuffing the skin with minced meat and spices, proud of how neatly it held together. He even made pilaf rice once, aromatic and nutty, hoping the scent alone might tempt Sion. It didn't. In fact, Sion never picked at a single thing his father had attempted cooking. But it didn't matter. His father tried anyway. Cooking became his quiet offering, a way of saying, *'I see you, even if you never take a bite.'*

He was allergic to almost everything. They'd learned that the hard way.

There was one time, a few years back, when they ate at a Chinese restaurant not far from town. Sion had never had pineapple before. It was part of the sweet and sour pork, and no one had noticed it on his plate. He picked it up with his fingers, no rice, just the golden fruit, and bit into it. His eyes lit up. For a moment, he looked surprised. Almost happy. He took another bite. Then another.

After the third one, something shifted.

His left eye began to swell. Then his lip, curling oddly on one side. He stopped eating. Said nothing. Just sat there with his spoon in his hand.

Someone nearby noticed. *"You need to call someone,"* they said. *"Is he alright?"*

But his parents didn't panic. His mother just placed her hand gently on his back. His father pushed the last bowl toward the middle of the table and reached for the bill.

They were already finished eating. Sion, even like that, wasn't struggling. No wheezing. No fear in his eyes. Just stillness.

They knew this kind of moment. They had lived through many. Hives, swelling, breath held too long. Doctors who didn't listen. Nurses who did. At some point, they stopped treating every reaction like an emergency. And Sion… he never did. He never cried or clutched at his throat or whimpered like he needed saving.

So they stood. Thanked the staff. Walked out of the restaurant calmly, as if they were stepping out into an ordinary afternoon.

They didn't explain. They didn't have to. There was something in the way they held themselves, tired, maybe, but sure. As though they'd made peace with the fact that their son didn't fit into anyone's categories. He wasn't breakable. He wasn't fragile. He was just… different. Different in a way no doctor could name, no test could show.

Later that evening, his mother gave him medicine. His father watched from the hallway, arms folded, quiet. They didn't speak about it.

Sion didn't ask. His face was half-swollen, but peaceful. He sat on the floor and began drawing again. His fingers steady. His breathing soft.

They didn't talk about how strange it was that he never panicked. That his body reacted but he never did.

They just watched him.

And somewhere inside, they both knew, he would be alright. He always was.

Most of Sion's time was spent drawing.

He used to draw only on paper, stacks of plain A4 sheets his mother kept in a box by the shelf. He'd go through them fast. Page after page. Sometimes filling both sides. But no matter what he drew, no matter how beautiful or strange, he always shredded them once he was done. Into strips. Neat, careful, like a ritual. He never explained why.

So one day, his father bought him an iPad. Not to replace the paper, but to stop the drawings from disappearing. He didn't say much, just left it on the table one morning with a note that read: *"Please save what you make."*

Sion didn't argue. He said thank you and started using it.

Not for games, he didn't care for those. Just for drawing. Sketch after sketch. Sometimes, he animated them, little figures moving just enough to feel alive. His fingers moved quick and sure, like they already knew what needed to be drawn before he did.

But even the iPad struggled to keep up. His mind raced faster than the screen could follow. There were nights when he'd fill a dozen layers and start over, as if the first ten versions weren't quite right. Other times, he slowed down. His lines became deliberate, careful. He created images with such precision, they looked printed, sometimes even alive.

He also made three-dimensional models. Full characters. Joints. Shadows. He animated them, gave them weight and movement. They were beautiful, but often unsettling. Things with hollow mouths, wide hands, too many knees. Like creatures from a place no one remembered.

Some nights, he made three-dimensional models on the screen, entire characters with joints, motion, light. He gave them breath and movement, blinking eyes, twisting shadows. They were beautiful, in their own way. But many were unsettling. Creatures that looked too human, or not quite enough. Long limbs, bent backs, empty mouths. Eerie, as if they came from a place that didn't want to be remembered.

Still, sometimes he'd just draw a cat. Soft fur, curled tail, big eyes. Nothing dark or strange, just a cat.

But Sion didn't have a cat. And when asked, he said he didn't want one.

Not because he didn't like them. He did. That was the problem.

"*They're too beautiful*," he whispered once. "I don't deserve things like that."

His father noticed, for years now, how often Sion drew cats. He'd sketch them on the edges of other drawings, sometimes whole pages filled with different poses. Now and then, he'd show one to his father with a faint smile, rare, quiet, but there. That was enough. So his father made a decision. He started searching quietly, without telling Sion. He found a post on Gumtree: a litter of ragdoll kittens, soft grey and white, with flecks of black above the eyes like faint brows. The youngest of the five caught his attention immediately, its tail darker than the rest, a little bundle of waiting. His wife wasn't convinced. She worried about the mess, the travel, the effort it would take, especially with everything else already in their hands. But his mind was set. This was something he could do. Something that might help.

On the day of the pickup, they waited outside the house for a while. Sion didn't speak. He rarely did. But his father knew to give him time. A few minutes to settle. To prepare. Finally, they walked to the door, his father leading, Sion a quiet step behind, and his mother trailing gently.

The woman who opened the door was tall and thin, her hands as delicate as branches. She smiled faintly, tilting her head like she, too, moved to some rhythm not everyone could hear. Greetings were made. Just then, from the dim hallway behind her, the kitten appeared. Quick, light-footed. It darted past her legs, past the father's shoes then stopped at Sion's feet. Pressed against him. Settled there like a heartbeat. The woman gasped, covering her mouth. *"He's never done that,"* she said. *"That one's always hiding when people come. He doesn't trust easily. He always runs to the far corner…"* She trailed off, still watching. But Sion didn't move. He just looked down. And for a moment, just a flicker, his shoulders softened. Like something heavy had shifted, just a little. They didn't need to say anything else. That was the cat. That was the one.

"We will call him PipSqueak," Sion whispered. Almost to himself. But that was enough

Both parents froze, wide-eyed, but only for a second. Then came the quick, breathless reply *"Yes,"* his father said. *"Yes, of course we will."*

His father had tried to give him gifts over the years, things other boys might love. Toys. A game station. A box of oil pastels. But Sion always pushed them away gently, never angry, just certain.

"You should give that to other kids," he whispered. "I'm not supposed to have things."

His father never hovered. He never pushed to be close. But he lingered more often in the doorway now, especially when Sion was sketching in silence. Watching, without watching. He'd sometimes ask simple things like *"Want something to drink?"* or *"Still working on that one?"* even if he didn't get a reply.

He'd stopped expecting answers.

He just kept showing up. Fixing things around the house. Making sure the rice was stocked. Buying spare paper or pens when he noticed the old ones wearing down. It wasn't loud love. It wasn't warm or overflowing. But it was steady. Always there. The kind of love that doesn't know how to say much but tries anyway.

And then there was his mother.

She carried her tenderness more openly, though quieter than most would notice. She folded his clothes a certain way. Brushed his hair even when he flinched. Sat beside him when he couldn't eat but wouldn't leave the table. She never asked why he whispered. Never begged him to speak louder.

She cried sometimes, but only when she was alone.

She remembered that night.

The call had come just after midnight. She was in the breakroom, eating leftover adobo from a plastic container, watching a nurse try to fix the vending machine again. Her phone buzzed once. Then again.

Her husband's voice on the other end wasn't panicked, but something in it made her drop her fork.

By the time she got down to A&E, they were already inside. Sion sat on the hospital bed, wrapped in a foil blanket, his hair damp, his socks gone. Her husband stood by the door, soaked up to the knees, like he'd waded through something too deep to explain.

The room smelled faintly of antiseptic and something cleaner than water.

She didn't ask questions. Didn't press the doctor who muttered words like "reaction" and "unusual presentation."

She just walked to her son, kissed his damp forehead, and sat beside him as if it were an ordinary thing to do.

But later that week, while folding the same shirt three times because her hands wouldn't stop shaking, she let herself remember it fully. The white water. The silence. The doctor's strange look.

And the quiet voice in her that whispered, he isn't like other children.

She had always known.

But that was the night she stopped wishing otherwise.

Late at night, in the fourth room with the glass window, she would sit and look out at the brook, the soft shimmer of water barely visible beneath the trees. And in that small silence, she would let herself feel it. The ache.

Sometimes it came as guilt. Other times, grief.

But most of the time, it was something quieter, a wish.

Not cruel or selfish. Just the soft kind, the tired kind. The kind that came when she saw other children at the shops laughing loudly, running with crisps in their hands. Sticky fingers, shouting nonsense, begging their mums for sweets.

And she would think, why can't he have that? Why can't I have that, just once?

She never told anyone. Not even her husband. But she felt it. That quiet yearning for something simple, something ordinary. A son who sang songs in the car. A boy who ran into her arms at the school gate.

But Sion wasn't that. He was never that.

He was something else entirely.

So she wiped her eyes, folded the washing, and packed another bowl of jasmine rice and cold Spam. Then she went to his room, knocked once, and left the tray by the table on the bedside, because that's what he needed.

And she loved him too much to wish he were different.

And then he'd go back to drawing.

He never looked people in the eye. Not even his parents. He wasn't being rude, he just couldn't. Eye contact felt too loud. Too sharp. So he looked down, or sideways, or not at all. But he noticed everything. The way his father's jaw tightened when bills arrived. The way his mother lingered a bit longer at the window when it rained.

Sion was most alive at night.

When the rest of the world settled into sleep, he would be up. Silent feet on the floorboards. Light tapping from his stylus on glass. Sometimes he sat in that empty room with the window. Sometimes he didn't move at all, just stared at the brook and let the dark wrap round him.

One morning, just as the sun began to blur through the leaves, his mother came into the room and saw what he had drawn.

It was a cage. Wire. Bent and uneven. Inside was a cat, white with one ginger paw. Its eyes wide, alert, pressed against the bars.

She didn't say anything. Just looked at it, then at him. Sion kept drawing, ignoring her. Or maybe he wasn't ignoring her. Maybe he just knew she didn't have the words for it.

That afternoon, a neighbour knocked.

"Have you seen Lulu?" she asked. *"Our cat's gone missing. White with a ginger paw."*

His mother glanced at Sion, still sitting on the sofa, tapping at his screen.

"No," she said. *"Haven't seen her."*

But her eyes said something else.

In the drawing, the cage sat in a dark space. No background. No door. No key.

And though he never spoke a word aloud, Sion whispered something that night as he looked out at the brook, watching the light catch the edges of the water.

No one heard it but the trees.

CHAPTER 2

The Wrong Kind Of Noise

School was the hardest part of the week.

The building always felt too big, like it was built for children who knew how to be loud. The corridors echoed with shouting, footsteps, chair legs scraping across floors. Bells rang without warning. The lights flickered. The smells changed from one room to the next, plastic, bleach, feet, burnt toast. It was all too much.

Sion moved through it like a shadow. Head down. Shoulders tight. He didn't speak unless he had to. Even then, it was in whispers no one could hear.

Teachers said things like *"You just need to try harder,"* or *"He's in his own little world,"* or sometimes, when they forgot to lower their voices, *"We're not really equipped for this."*

They meant well. Most of them.

But they didn't see the way the fluorescent lights buzzed like angry bees in his ears. They didn't feel how sharp the carpet was under his palms when he pressed his hands to the floor to ground himself. They didn't understand how a single pencil dropping on the other side of the room could make his chest go tight.

One morning, during literacy, a supply teacher asked Sion to read aloud. He didn't look up. Didn't move. The room had gone quiet. The teacher repeated his name, then sighed, said, *"Come on now, don't be rude."* A few classmates laughed.

He tried. Opened his mouth. But nothing came out.

He couldn't speak in front of all those eyes. His voice didn't work that way. The supply teacher marked it down as *"Defiant behaviour."* It went in the system, next to all the other notes he never read.

So he hid.

Under tables. Behind coats. Inside the disabled toilet with the lock turned but not clicked. He didn't cause trouble. He just vanished, quietly, into smaller spaces. Safer ones.

There was one teacher who tried. Mr Henson. He had soft shoes that didn't squeak when he walked. He spoke slowly, not like the others. And he never asked Sion questions out loud in front of the class.

One day, he placed a small rubber toy on Sion's desk, one of those squeeze things with little beads inside. No instructions. No pressure. Just left it there and walked away. Sion held it under the desk for the rest of the day. It helped.

But kindness in the classroom didn't stop cruelty in the corridors.

The other children didn't understand Sion. And children, when they don't understand something, don't often leave it alone.

They called him names. Whispered them at first, then louder when they saw he didn't respond. They'd tap the back of his chair or flick things at his feet when the teacher wasn't looking. In the lunch hall, they moved their trays away from his. In the playground, they ran around him in circles shouting nonsense, laughing at how he never shouted back.

Sion carried a blue bag. Worn at the edges, heavy with his drawings. Little toys dangled from every side, odd shapes, tiny animals, soft loops and plastic beads. Each one meant something. A sound he remembered. A time he felt calm. A story only he understood. They helped him focus when the world was too much.

One afternoon on the field, Callum grabbed the bag hard from Sion's shoulder. It yanked him sideways. Sion stumbled but didn't fall. The bag hit the ground. Papers spilled out across the grass. The toys bounced and scattered.

Callum laughed at first. He picked up one of the pages, maybe expecting something silly.

But then he froze.

The drawing was sharp. Detailed. Almost real. And it showed Callum, standing exactly as he was, gripping the blue bag.

His own face was drawn too. But the eyes looked strange. Wild. Like they'd seen something too late.

Callum stared at it for a full second. Then another. Then his hand began to shake. He dropped the page and stepped back.

Then he ran.

Full speed. Across the field. No words.

His mates called after him. *"Oi, what's wrong?"* *"Callum?"* *"Where are you going?"*

But none of them followed.

Not at first.

Then one boy looked down at the scattered drawings.

And then he ran too.

And the others, confused, nervous, sensing something they couldn't explain, they followed. Shouting. Laughing uneasily. But running all the same.

Sion didn't move. He sat in the grass, mud on his trousers, tears on his face. Not loud sobs, just steady, quiet weeping, like something inside had given up asking to be heard.

He gathered what drawings he could. Not all of them. Just a few. The rest were left behind, fluttering like fallen leaves.

He didn't understand why he was like this. Why sounds were knives and lights were hammers. Why he couldn't speak properly, or play the way they did. He wanted to be like them. Truly, he did. To shout silly things and run and be part of the noise.

But he couldn't.

He couldn't fake himself.

Callum didn't come back to school the next day. Or the day after that.

No one said why. There were no announcements. No notes sent round. Just an empty chair with his name still stuck to the edge of the table, peeling slightly at the corner.

His mates, normally loud, always joking, had gone quiet. They didn't laugh the same. They didn't talk about the field. They didn't mention the bag, or the drawings, or the way Callum had looked when he ran.

They just… stopped.

Mr Henson must have noticed. He watched the group closely that week, but he didn't say much either. Maybe he sensed that something had happened but didn't know how to reach it. Or maybe, deep down, he knew that if it involved Sion, it wouldn't come out easily, not in words.

What happened that day didn't get shared in the playground. It didn't turn into one of those wild stories that grows and mutates as it spreads. It didn't become a joke. It wasn't bragged about.

Instead, it slipped into that quiet category of things children *don't* talk about. Not because they were told not to, but because they couldn't. Because something about it didn't sit right. Didn't make sense.

Because none of them could explain what it was, or what they'd seen, or why it made their stomach twist just remembering it.

Even Callum, when he returned the following week, wasn't the same.

He didn't look at Sion. Not once. He kept his distance. He stopped grabbing people's bags, stopped flicking pencils, stopped sneering when others stumbled through a sentence. The boys who used to trail behind him didn't follow as close anymore. Something had shifted.

They didn't fear Sion, not exactly. But there was something about him now they wouldn't go near.

Whatever they felt on the field that day, whatever chilled them, whatever unsettled them, it stayed with them.

They didn't have the words for it. But they remembered.

And Sion, as always, said nothing.

He just watched. And kept drawing.

His father was already waiting outside when the bell rang.

He always was.

Private cars weren't allowed in the school's pick-up zone, only the buses could pull in, so his father parked just outside the fence, across from the tall grasses that lined the edge of the field. The Polestar 2 was easy to spot, low and quiet, with its clean, sharp design. It barely made a sound when it rolled up.

He arrived fifteen minutes early. Every time. On the dot. Quarter to three.

Work could always wait. He told his team that from the start. He did everything from home anyway—remote IT work, mostly. The sort that stayed on screens and in code. But even when the projects piled up or the calls dragged on, he never let the clock slip past.

Now he sat in the driver's seat, elbow rested against the window, eyes fixed on the school fence. He didn't need a clear view. Even through the metal bars and the shifting sunlight, even behind the tall grass, if a shadow passed that moved like Sion, he would know.

The weather was kind that day. September light, soft and low. The sky was open and dry, the air not too cold yet. Just enough crisp in it to suggest autumn was near, but still warm on the skin.

He considered asking Sion if they could stop at the park on the way home. Just a short walk. Sion liked the park, the stretch of winding trail near the back, the rows of quiet trees, the little stream with smooth stones and shallow ripples.

When Sion finally appeared, his shoulders looked tired. The usual way. But his feet moved steadily, not dragging, and his face didn't show anything that would worry his father, though Sion's face rarely showed much at all.

He got in the car without speaking. Buckled in.

His father didn't ask about the day. He never did, unless Sion started it first. But as they pulled away, he said, *"It's nice out. Want to walk a bit? Just the park."*

Sion nodded.

So they drove a few minutes to the little car park at the entrance of Roath Park, a patch of green tucked between the estates and the lower hills. A place not many people went on weekdays. Not loud. Not crowded. Just quiet.

The trees were starting to shift colours, but only just. Most still held onto their greens, with a few branches dusted in amber and rust. Sion walked slowly, hands in his pockets, eyes tracing the lines of the ground where sticks snapped beneath his feet and dry leaves flitted sideways in the breeze.

They passed a wooden footbridge, the kind with creaky planks and moss in the corners. Underneath, the stream flowed, thin but steady. Clear. Gentle. Sion stopped to watch it for a moment. He didn't smile, but he tilted his head the way he always did when something caught his attention.

He crouched for a bit, touched a flat stone, then stayed still, staring at the water.

The stream moved slowly, threading its way between mossy rocks and fallen twigs. Sunlight touched the surface in thin silver lines, and tiny bubbles gathered near the banks. Leaves floated past, some yellow, some still green, spinning in soft circles before slipping away. The current was shallow, but steady. The kind of water that seemed to remember everything it touched.

His father watched from the bridge above.

It wasn't anything Sion said, he hadn't spoken since getting in the car, but there was something in the way he crouched. The stillness of it. The way he stared too long at the water, like he wasn't looking at the stream, but *through* it.

Like he was somewhere else entirely.

His father stayed quiet. Just watched. He thought of asking *Is everything alright? Did something happen at school?*. but the questions caught in his throat.

He knew that if Sion wanted to tell him, he would.

So he stood there, letting the quiet settle around them like fallen leaves.

And when Sion finally stood up and walked on, his father followed.

Just a step behind.

His father walked behind, not too close, not too far. Just enough.

Birds moved through the higher branches, robins or finches, small and fast. A dog barked faintly in the distance, but not near enough to disturb the quiet.

The path curved round a low bend, then split near a weeping willow. Sion took the left fork, the one that led back toward the car park. On the right was ice cream van. His father was about to ask if he wanted an ice cream with the chocolate stick on it, that's what Sion would usually want. But his father didn't because he thought Sion would normally just ask if ever he wants one. Sion had had enough walking for the day.

They didn't speak on the way home. And when they arrived, Sion went straight inside. Left his bag by the stairs. Took off his shoes. Washed his hands. The same way he always did.

His mother was already by the door, smiling, always. When she wasn't working, she waited for him like that every day. First, she'd peek from the kitchen window the moment the Blink doorbell announced him, once from the gate, then again at the front door. And no matter what she was doing, chopping, folding, halfway through a call, she'd drop it in a heartbeat just to be there when he stepped in. She kissed his head gently, like she always did, even if he didn't react. That moment was hers. A quiet joy she never missed.

The house was quiet, but never unwatched.

Sion's father had filled it with cameras, more than ten, just Blink alone. Some were tucked in plain sight: one by the gate, one angled just above the front steps, two inside the hallway ceiling. Others were hidden, placed so subtly even his wife wasn't sure where they all were. But she didn't mind. She knew it wasn't about paranoia. It was about protection. Keeping Sion safe. Watching for the things he couldn't always name.

There were screens everywhere, by the front door, above the fridge, in the small lounge near the Wi-Fi router. Most days, they flickered with motion-detected snapshots: cars passing, birds landing, a neighbour's cat sneaking through the hedge. But when Sion was out, those screens became lifelines. His father monitored them with quiet precision, eyes scanning each frame like reading code. It wasn't obsessive. It was instinct. The kind of vigilance that came from years of not knowing what could happen next and needing to be ready, just in case.

Sion didn't mention the field. He didn't say anything about Callum. Or the drawings. Or the way the others had run.

Sion went straight to his room.

That evening, at home, he drew.

Not a creature this time. Not a cage.

A staircase. Narrow. Shadowed. And under it, the girl. Knees pulled to her chest. Hair tangled. Eyes red.

It wasn't from memory. He hadn't seen her like that. Not in school. Not anywhere.

But when it was finished, he stared at the drawing for a long time. He felt something in his chest, tight and quiet, like something was stuck there.

He didn't show it to anyone. Just saved it and closed the app.

A week later, Mr Henson took the girl outside during morning break. She was crying. Sion watched from the window. He couldn't hear anything, but he saw Mr Henson crouch down beside her and place a hand on her back, just like his mother did.

Later, they said she'd been hurting at home. That someone finally told.

Sion didn't react. He just kept drawing.

But that night, he couldn't sleep. The house was quiet, the kind of quiet that should've been peaceful, but wasn't. He sat in the fourth room and stared out into the dark, the brook half-visible through bare branches. The wind moved gently. Leaves whispered against the glass.

And he whispered, too.

Not words. Just breath and thought and feeling. A soft letting go.

Somewhere far away, a girl slept under a safer roof.

Chapter 3
The Foods That Don't Hurt

There were arguments in the kitchen again.

Not shouting. They never did. Just tired voices, rising and falling behind a half-shut door. The kind of argument that had been said before. One that didn't need new words.

"He needs more than this and too much rice or chocolate is bad for him," his father said.

"I know," his mother replied, scraping something into a bowl. *"But what do you want me to do? He only eats rice and Spam."*

"He's growing. He needs variety. Protein. Veg. He can't live like that forever."

There was a pause. A clatter of cutlery in the sink.

"He's not doing it to be difficult."

"I didn't say he was."

Outside the door, Sion sat quietly on the floor, legs crossed, sketchpad in hand. He wasn't drawing anything in particular, just lines. Curves. Loops. Spirals. Overlapping shapes like muscle or wire.

It wasn't that he didn't care what they were saying. He did. But he couldn't stop the shapes from forming. His hand kept moving, even as their voices carried on.

His body may have been still, but something inside him wasn't.

Upstairs, in his room, the bowl still sat untouched. Jasmine rice. Warm Spam. Exactly how he liked it.

His father didn't understand.

He tried. Truly. He loved Sion. But this, this quiet defiance of normality left him unsure. He worked in systems. Logic. Bugs and fixes. He wanted answers. He wanted solutions.

But Sion had none to give.

There had been too many attempts. Bits of chicken wrapped in breadcrumbs. Spoons of mashed sweet potato. One time, a colourful jelly. Each trial ended the same way. Staring. Silence. Then walking away.

They had taken him to specialists when he was younger. Nutritionists. Behavioural therapists. Allergy consultants. All of them wrote things down. None of them had answers that helped.

He wasn't just picky. He was protecting himself.

They knew this now.

Most days, his mother gave in. Not because she was weak, but because she was tired of seeing him suffer. She'd tried all the advice: change the shape of the food, use fun colours, present it like a game. None of it worked.

So she did what mothers do best when nothing else works, she made peace with it.

Rice and Spam.

Warm. In the white bowl. Always on the tray.

There was safety in sameness. A pattern his body could trust.

But it wasn't just preference. It was protection.

Sion's allergies weren't mild. They could be brutal. Swelling. Rashes. Itching in his throat that made him scratch at his neck until it bled. Once, even the steam from boiling prawns in the neighbour's flat had made him dizzy.

Seafood was dangerous. So were nuts, eggs, sometimes even fruits.

Once, it was grapes. Another time, just the smell of tangerine peel.

There was always a new threat, some tiny enemy hiding inside what others called food.

Sometimes, when things got tense in the house, when Sion wouldn't eat for days except his cold rice and Spam, his father would drive out and come back with a box of KFC. Never said why. Just placed it on the table. His mother always smiled faintly, the same way she did in the hospital years ago when friends brought chicken while she was delivering Sion. It had been her favourite then, a smell that reminded her of long drives in Southampton, windows down, streets loud with life. No one ate much that day. But the bucket stayed between them, warm, grounding. A strange anchor in a sea of unknowns.

Now, even years later, his father sometimes brought it home, not for Sion, who wouldn't touch it, but as a quiet ritual. A way of saying: we've been here before. We'll be okay.

He also remembered the time his mother tried to add chopped carrots into his rice. She thought if she diced them small enough, he wouldn't notice. But he had. The colour alone made his stomach twist. He cried, not out of tantrum, but panic. His body had already decided it didn't feel safe.

He pressed both hands over his ears and lay flat on the floor, rocking until the taste left his mouth.

They never tried carrots again.

There was one night, years ago, that neither of them spoke about anymore.

Sion had been just six then.

His father had stayed up late, a glass or two more than he meant to. Nothing heavy, just enough to blur the edges. The house was quiet, and he'd almost nodded off on the sofa when a sound snapped him back.

A retching noise. Repeating. Wet and hollow. It came from Sion's room.

He stumbled off the sofa, still dizzy, still thick in the head. But what he found sobered him quick.

Sion was standing in the middle of his room, head tilted back, eyes closed. And from his mouth—water. Pouring out. Arcing up in a smooth, eerie curve and falling over him like a fountain. It wasn't vomit in the usual sense. It was white, like milk, but thinner, clearer. Too clean. Odourless.

The sound of it hitting the floor was soft, rhythmic. There was already a pool soaking the carpet. The whole room glistened, quiet and bright under the bedside lamp. It was like watching something unreal. A dream.

His father froze.

It had been going on for minutes already.

When it finally stopped, Sion began to breathe again. Quick. Light. Not gasping, not distressed, just as if something had left him and now there was space again.

His father rushed to him then, lifted his small, soaked body off the floor and shouted into his phone. An ambulance came in under ten minutes.

On the way, he called his wife.

She was working the night shift at the same hospital.

They never figured out what it was. The doctors called it a severe allergic reaction. But it didn't explain the volume. The force. The stillness in Sion's face. Or the way the room looked after, like nothing had really happened.

No sour smell. No panic.

Just silence. And water.

Sion was back to his drawing like nothing happened.

That afternoon, his father sat at the far end of the lounge, a half-drunk cup of coffee in his hands. It had gone cold long ago, but he held it still, turning the mug slowly between his palms.

He hadn't said much that day.

The autumn light came through the window, laying soft shadows on the floor. Sion was in his room, quiet, as always. His footsteps had creaked the hallway floorboards earlier, and now nothing.

Sion's father looked up at the ceiling, at a spot just above the hallway door—and stayed there a moment too long. His wife noticed. Said nothing.

He blinked, lowered his eyes, and set the mug down gently. The porcelain clicked on wood. Then he stood, stretched his back, and walked toward the kitchen without a word.

His silence wasn't new. But it held something different that day. Not worry. Not dread.

Something remembered.

That afternoon, while his parents sat in the lounge—his father silent, scrolling half-heartedly on his laptop—Sion sat cross-legged in the spare room with the glass window.

He was drawing again.

This time, not lines or shadows.

A creature.

It had a wide mouth. Not just one, but many. Stacked, like layers of paper cut jagged down the middle. Each one opened differently. Some sharp. Some round. Some crooked.

Its body was coiled like intestines, wrapped tight, bloated. Its eyes were small and deep, far back in its head, like they were retreating.

The creature didn't move. But it looked like it had eaten too much. Or never stopped eating. Its many mouths reminded him of noise, constant chewing, swallowing, gnashing.

It made him feel sick, but he couldn't stop drawing it.

He didn't name it.

But when his father passed by the room and glanced at the screen, he stopped.

He didn't say anything. Just looked for a moment longer than usual.

The eyes. The eyes of the creature. They were familiar.

He didn't want to believe it. But he knew.

They were his own.

Chapter 4

Things He Sees That Aren't There

Gloucestershire was darker than Sion expected. Not night-dark, but something heavier. Denser. Like the shadows had mass.

They were visiting a close family friend, someone his mother had known since they joined a small charismatic group. It was a long drive from Circle Wood. His father insisted on leaving late to avoid traffic, but now it was nearing midnight, and they were still on the road.

They had just passed a sign that read *Cotswolds Area of Outstanding Natural Beauty*, though there was nothing visible in the pitch black to prove it. The national road stretched on like a ribbon of quiet black water, no streetlights, no passing cars, just the low hum of the tyres rolling across tarmac.

The road was narrow, hemmed in by tall hedges and wild grass that brushed the edges of the car doors. Behind the grass stood crooked trees, thin, reaching things that tangled together overhead like a cathedral made of bark and silence. Their branches moved stiffly in the wind, and once in a while the car lights would catch a pale trunk or a patch of moss, and it looked like a face. Then gone.

Sion sat in the back seat, pressed against the window, fingers lightly tapping on the glass. He wasn't drawing. He wasn't doing anything, really. Just watching. Eyes half-lidded, body still. The seatbelt tugged at his shoulder with every turn.

No one was speaking. The music had been turned off miles ago. Only the sound of tyres, the occasional creak of the chassis, and the faint tick of the indicator when his father overtook a slow lorry earlier.

Then Sion whispered.

So softly that only the night heard it.

His mother turned to look at him. *"Did you say something, anak?"*

But Sion didn't answer. He was still looking out the window. Focused. Not blinking.

His father caught the look in the rear-view mirror. *"He alright?"* he asked.

"I think so."

But she wasn't sure. Because now Sion's hand had moved to the glass, tracing something with his fingertip. Slowly. As if following the outline of something only he could see.

And the car slowed slightly.

Because up ahead, in the distance, something was on the road.

It looked like a person. At first.

But then it shifted.

Sion's eyes stayed on the glass, unblinking. His finger stopped moving.

In the front seat, his mother's phone slipped from the dashboard holder. It hit the centre console with a dull thud and slid down into the narrow gap by the gear stick.

"Ah—hold on," his father muttered, glancing down.

He reached between the seats, fumbling. The car veered slightly to the left. He corrected it quickly with one hand on the wheel, but didn't look up straight away.

"I'll get it," his wife offered, already reaching down. But he was quicker.

"No, I've got it."

He wedged two fingers into the space and tried to pinch the edge of the phone. It was stubborn. Plastic against plastic. His knuckles knocked the gear and the hazard light switch. He swore softly under his breath.

The car dipped gently over a rise, tyres humming. Still no one else on the road.

Then Sion leaned forward.

His chin nearly touched the seatbelt.

And his voice came, just a whisper.

"Don't look up yet."

But his father did.

Just as his fingers caught the edge of the phone and lifted it from the crevice, his eyes flicked up to the road.

And that's when he saw it.

A shape. Towering. Bent forward, arms too long. Its shoulders reached both sides of the road, thin but sprawling. It had no face, not properly, only a smooth stretch where features should've been, like wax melted and pulled down. One foot stepped forward, but made no sound. The knees bent the wrong way.

It didn't move like it belonged here. It didn't move like it belonged anywhere.

The father gasped, sharp and sudden. The car jerked violently right, tyres screaming against gravel. His wife screamed his name.

He swerved, hard. Right wheel into the grass, front bumper catching air for half a second as the car bounced off the edge and back onto the road. He slammed the brakes. The vehicle slid to a stop.

Silence.

Nothing on the road. No creature. No shape. Nothing at all.

He sat frozen, knuckles white on the wheel, heart thudding against the inside of his ribs. His wife stared at him, then looked out the front window. Only darkness. Tall trees. Empty tarmac.

She turned to the back seat.

Sion hadn't moved. His hands rested quietly on his lap. But his eyes, they were still fixed on the spot ahead. As if whatever was there hadn't fully gone.

Her voice shook. *"Did you see?"*

"Someone," the father said, still breathless. *"Something. I don't"* He wiped his face with one hand. *"It was just a second. Like a shadow."*

"A shadow with arms?" she whispered.

They didn't answer.

Sion whispered something then, so low it barely carried.

But his father heard it.

"It wasn't for you."

They didn't speak much after that. The car stayed quiet, save for the low hum of the tyres and the occasional blink of the indicator as they turned onto quieter roads. The trees thinned, the air felt colder, and before long they reached the edge of the village, stone cottages softened by moss and time.

Their friends lived just beyond it, in a converted barn tucked behind a long gravel drive. This was their first visit. They'd meant to come for years but never had the time. Now it was nearly midnight.

The porch light was on when they arrived, casting long yellow streaks onto the gravel. The house stood tall and dark behind it, old wood and clean brick wrapped in ivy. A warm glow flickered through the windows.

The couple stepped out to greet them, laughing, kind, a little shy. The man waved from the door. The woman opened her arms for a hug, but paused as she saw Sion.

They knew. The parents had explained beforehand. That he didn't like being touched. That he might not speak. That he sometimes didn't make eye contact, but still noticed everything.

But Sion surprised them.

He walked up slowly, without a word, and reached for their hands. One at a time, he took each of their right hands gently in his own and pressed them to his forehead. A small bow of his head. A quiet offering.

It was "*mano*," his mother whispered, smiling. A Filipino gesture. A mark of respect to the elders.

Their hosts looked moved. Not sure what to say.

Inside, the house smelled of cinnamon and soft wood. Low lamps, thick rugs, books in piles. The kind of place that felt lived in. Safe. Familiar.

But Sion was cautious. He made his calculations, he always did. He scanned the layout, the ceilings, the corners, the exits. His breathing stayed shallow. His eyes darted but didn't settle.

Then, without a word, he moved to the far end of the living room and sat.

Not in the centre. Never there.

He perched on the very edge of the sofa, where the arm met the wall. A spot just out of the way. Tucked. Cocooned.

His mother took a seat nearby. His father followed, chatting politely with their friends. There was tea, and quiet talk about the drive.

Sion said nothing.

But he reached for his iPad, pulled it from his bag, and began to draw.

His finger moved quick, tapping, dragging. Zooming in and out. Layers stacked. Erased. Redrawn. He leaned close, almost nose to the screen, his whole posture folding inward.

He stayed like that for an hour.

While the grown-ups talked, he sat still, breathing slow, fingers gliding across glass like they were remembering something. Or conjuring something.

That night, as Sion sat hunched over his iPad, PipSqueak climbed softly onto the foot of his bed. The cat rarely meowed, almost as quiet as Sion himself. But he always knew where to be.

When Sion's hand trembled mid-sketch, PipSqueak placed a paw near his ankle—just enough weight to remind him he was here, and still whole. The creature he'd been drawing began to shrink on the screen, its long claws softening into branches. Its eyes dulled. Then vanished.

Sometimes, the cat helped him finish what he couldn't do alone.

The iPad glowed softly in the guest room, casting pale blue light across his blanket. His parents were asleep down the hall. He was curled on the mattress by the floor, not in the bed. He preferred it that way, close to the carpet. Near the door.

And on the screen…

A long road stretched through darkness.

Tall grasses on either side. A single car in the middle.

Above it, bent in the sky like a question mark, was the creature.

He hadn't drawn it fully.

Only the arms. The curve of the back. The faint shimmer of something falling from its hand.

He stared at it for a while.

Then, slowly, he swiped to a new canvas.

And started drawing a face.

Not the creature's.

His own.

The next morning, he was quiet. More than usual.

He didn't touch his breakfast. He didn't draw either. Just sat near the window and watched the ivy curl down the wall outside. His fingers tapped against his knees in a rhythm that made no sense to anyone else.

His mother noticed. She didn't press.

On the way home, he started drawing again. This time not on the iPad, but with his finger on the fogged-up glass of the window. Not shapes exactly. Not creatures.

Just a single circle.

Then another. And another.

Each one slightly misshapen, slightly off-centre. Eyes maybe. Or heads. Or burdens too heavy to be carried.

When they got home, he headed straight to the corner of the fourth room and curled up by the window. No words. No dinner.

He drew all night.

This time, the creature was different.

It had no face. Just a heavy blur where features should've been. The hands were long and soft. Not sharp, not dangerous. But trembling, as if holding something it couldn't name.

Behind it, shadows bled from a woman's back.

The woman wasn't real. Not someone he knew.

But she looked like she could be anyone. A teacher. A mother. A stranger in a shop queue.

Her mouth was closed, her body folded inward like paper.

Above her head hovered a single word:

"Sorry."

That Sunday, they travelled west to Merthyr Tydfil.

It was a long drive, quiet for the most part. Sion didn't speak. He just watched the fields slide past. His father was invited to give a talk at a small charismatic gathering. The topic: forgiveness.

The venue was tucked beneath a parish church, a modest hall with clean brick walls and a row of narrow windows only on south side of the hall. Fresh chairs lined the floor. A table of biscuits and tea stood in the corner. Almost at the centre of the hall stretches two tables holding trays of food. The place smelled of new carpets and air freshener. But it was warm. Welcoming.

Sion stayed at the right side of the hall, behind a square column with a small table. No one else could see him from where he sat, not the audience, not the service team but his father could. Just barely. From the lectern, his father had a direct line of sight to that narrow space where Sion perched like a shadow.

There were paintings on the walls, stations of the cross, portraits of saints. But the one that caught Sion's attention was Rembrandt's *The Return of the Prodigal Son*. It hung just slightly off-centre, near the end of the room. Dimly lit, but visible.

Sion was staring at it.

Or so it seemed.

Expressionless, unmoving, his gaze fixed in that direction.

His father glanced over mid-sentence, catching a flicker in Sion's eyes. But something didn't feel right. It wasn't the painting he was looking at.

Just beside it, seated quietly on a metal folding chair, was a woman.

She was part of the community. Middle-aged. Softspoken. She had introduced herself earlier and sat alone for most of the session, her hands clasped together in her lap.

At first, his father didn't think anything of it.

But then it hit him.

The slumped shoulders. The shape of the hair. The tilt of the chin. She looked exactly like the woman in Sion's drawing the night before. The same weariness pressed into her posture. The same silent weight.

He wasn't looking at the painting.

He was looking through her.

At the closing of the talk was a group sharing.

They divided into four smaller circles across the hall, each group huddled in quiet conversation. Chairs creaked softly as people leaned in. Voices dropped to a hush. The kind of setting where secrets sometimes slip out.

Sion's father excused himself and wandered into the small kitchen near the back. It had a square opening in the wall, half-window, half-hatch, that looked straight into the main hall. From there, he could see everyone.

He made himself a cup of coffee. Black. No sugar. The kettle clicked off with a soft metallic pop, and he stirred it absent-mindedly while watching the groups.

Then he saw her.

The woman from earlier, Sion's drawing made real.

She was speaking to her group now. Her voice low but shaking. One hand gripped the back of her chair; the other covered her face. She wasn't loud. She didn't wail. But even from the kitchen, he could see her shoulders trembling.

Her pain was quiet. Contained.

But real.

Exactly how it had been in the sketch. The posture, the hidden face, the way her foot curled beneath the chair, every detail matched.

He stood frozen for a moment, coffee forgotten in his hands.

And then, something even more unexpected happened.

From the edge of the hall, Sion moved.

Slow, small steps. No sound. He approached the woman gently, without interrupting the group. He didn't say a word. Just walked up to her, holding a folded piece of paper in both hands.

She looked up.

He gave her the drawing.

And then turned away.

His father stared from the kitchen, unable to move. His heart beat hard in his chest, but not from fear. From awe. From the quiet strangeness of the moment.

Because that drawing wasn't from today.

It was from the night before.

The woman held the drawing in her lap. Her tears didn't stop, but something in her posture shifted, like something heavy had been named, finally. Not explained. Not solved. Just… seen.

Sion returned to his seat by the column. Picked up his iPad. Kept drawing, as if nothing had happened. As if he hadn't just handed a stranger a piece of her sorrow, shaped and shaded before it even showed.

His father didn't speak of it on the drive home. Sion sat quiet in the back, watching the trees blur past. The headlights caught dust and fog in their beams. The silence in the car felt full, not empty.

And though the words never left his mouth, Sion whispered something to himself again that night.

A name. A date. A shape.

No one heard it but the dark.

CHAPTER 5

He Doesn't Sleep At Night

Sion didn't sleep like most children.

Even as a toddler, he kept odd hours. His parents had tried all the usual things, warm milk, hot chocolate, soft lights, lullabies in slow Tagalog, but nothing worked. Now, they simply let him be. The house grew used to his movements at night: the soft creak of floorboards, the gentle tapping on glass, the low hum of his iPad charging by the socket.

He didn't make noise. Just existed in the quiet.

While the rest of the world rested, Sion seemed most alert. Awake in a way that didn't feel restless. He wasn't bored. He wasn't fidgeting like children do when they want to be somewhere else. He was *present*. Calm. Moving through the dark with the patience of someone who had nowhere else to be but here.

His favourite place at night was the fourth room, the one with the big window and view of the brook. In daylight, the glass reflected the sky. But at night, it turned the world inside out. It showed you yourself. The dim outline of your face against a deeper dark.

Sion would sit in front of it for long stretches of time, still as a photograph.

Sometimes he drew, soft strokes on the screen, his body folded gently over his knees. Other times he just watched. Not out the window, but into it. Like there was something inside the glass.

Something *behind* it.

The night is when Sion's mind wanders and it's in that drifting that things come into focus. He sees clearly what most people choose not to. The ache behind shut doors. Children with empty stomachs crying quietly into the dark. The moans of the homeless sleeping rough on Queen Street, their pain dragging across the pavement like a long sigh. He doesn't just imagine it. He hears it. All of it. The cold weight of unfairness. The sharp sting of being forgotten.

Sometimes, that's why you'd catch him staring into nothing because he wasn't really here. Not all the way. His body stayed by the window, but his mind wandered down alleys he'd never seen, into houses he'd never lived in, to people he'd never met. He carried their grief like it was his own.

The voices came louder at night.

They weren't in the room, but they filled it. Dull thuds in his chest. Sharp tugs behind his eyes. It was like walking into the middle of a crowded street where no one spoke aloud, but everyone was screaming on the inside.

He sat on the floor of the fourth room, legs tucked in, face turned toward the window but not seeing anything outside. Just dark. And inside that dark, he felt it.

A girl somewhere, fists clenched around a school jumper that didn't fit. Her mouth shut so tightly it trembled. A boy too scared to go home, his eyes swollen from hiding tears. A woman folding laundry in the quiet, not noticing the bruise blooming on her collarbone.

Their pain buzzed through him like electricity.

His chest tightened.

He reached under his sleeve, fingers pressing the inside of his arm. Just to feel something here. Something now.

He pressed harder.

There was a snap of breath as the skin gave way, a sharp, thin sting. He didn't cry out. He never did. But the feeling travelled through him like a thread pulling taut, then unravelling.

The noise softened.

The girl breathed easier. The boy's fists unclenched. The woman blinked like someone had shaken her gently awake.

And Sion, he breathed in all their ache. Felt it throb through his wrist, pulsing into the skin. It settled there, like water soaking through fabric. Slow. Heavy.

He looked down at his arm. Blood pooled in a pinprick line, then curved.

He pulled his sleeve down.

Not to hide it.

To keep it safe.

He sat on the floor by the window, knees pulled close. The house was quiet now, but not empty. Not to him.

The argument downstairs had ended an hour ago, but the voices still echoed. His father's sharp tone. His mother's silence, then her crying. That part stayed with him the most, not the shouting, but the quiet that followed. The kind of silence that felt like something had been broken and no one knew how to fix it.

He'd seen her after. She was sitting on the end of the bed, facing away from the door. Her shoulders shaking a little. Not loud. Just tired. She held one of Sion's drawings in her hand, the corner damp from her thumb.

He didn't speak. Just stood in the hallway and watched. Then turned back to his room.

That's when the heaviness started. Like a slow drip filling the space around him. Not panic. Not sadness. Just weight. He could feel it in his arms, behind his eyes, in the tightness of his chest. It wasn't his, not really. It was hers. His mum's pain, sitting heavy in her lungs. His father's regret, twisting behind clenched teeth.

And more, people he didn't know, not really. A man curled on cardboard near Queen Street. A child in a grey hoodie crying into their knees in some quiet room he'd never seen. It all bled into him. And he didn't know how to make it stop.

So he reached for the inside of his arm.

At first, just a press of fingers. A pinch, sharp enough to feel. But it wasn't enough. The noise stayed.

Harder this time. Nails digging in.

Then again.

A jolt of pain. And suddenly, something shifted. The room grew quieter. Not outside, but inside. The swirl of sorrow dulled, like turning the volume down on a storm. The pressure eased. He felt... steadier.

The pain had gone somewhere. Moved out of them. Into him.

He pulled down his sleeve and looked away.

His arm throbbed, red and already starting to welt. But the air was still now. The heaviness lighter.

He didn't cry. He just lay back, hand resting gently over the mark.

He didn't know why it worked. Only that it did.

That was the first time it bled.

And it wouldn't be the last.

Each time he pinched his skin, it was for someone else. The pain they could no longer bear, he took it. Quietly. Without asking. A crying child. A woman pressed into silence. A boy bullied into bitterness. It flowed into him, unnoticed. The pinch drew it out of them and into his body, like water down a hidden drain.

His arms showed the cost. Pale marks in neat rows. Some scars flared red and angry. Others had faded into soft ghosts of what they once were. But none were accidental. Each one carried a name. A moment. A memory he couldn't forget.

That's why he wore long sleeves, even in warm weather. Not to hide shame. But to protect what no one else could see, wounds that weren't his, and pain that was no longer theirs.

There were nights when his parents would check on him, just to see if he was warm, if he'd eaten. His mother would peer into the room and see him motionless, staring at nothing. But when she asked, *"You alright, anak?"* he'd whisper something too soft to catch. Then go right back to watching.

Once, he sat there for almost four hours. Didn't blink much. Didn't draw a thing.

And on one of those nights, he saw it.

It didn't feel like a dream. And it wasn't his memory.

It began like a fog creeping through the window frame. The room remained as it was, but *somehow*, it changed. Light thinned. The air turned grey. The hum of the fridge down the hall disappeared.

In its place: the distant thud of boots on cobbled streets. A whistle in the wind. A voice shouting in a language not quite English. Not quite anything he knew.

Then, a girl.

She stood alone at the end of a narrow street. Rubble spilled around her. Dust hung in the air like ghosts. Her dress was torn at the shoulder, too big for her, stained near the hem. One shoe on, one shoe off. She was maybe seven. Maybe ten. Hard to tell in the gloom.

She wasn't crying. Not loudly. But her face was red. Her hands clutched something in her arms, a bundle wrapped in cloth.

Sion watched from the window, frozen. He didn't draw. He didn't whisper. Just watched.

The girl looked around, as if hearing something. Then she looked straight at him.

Straight *through* the glass.

And then she was gone.

The sound returned in a rush: the tick of the heater, the distant cough of a fox, the faint buzz of the electricity running through the wall.

Sion sat back.

His fingers trembled.

He didn't sleep that night.

Not because he couldn't.

But because he didn't *need* to.

Not yet.

CHAPTER 6
The Girl with the Red Coat

The house in Bristol was warm, full of familiar voices and quiet laughter. It belonged to one of the leaders, kind, migrated from Bahrain, with frames on the wall placed unevenly on every side of the wall. The scent of brewed coffee lingering through the main room. They had prepared a space upstairs for Sion, knowing he'd need somewhere quiet.

He didn't want to go at first. Stood near the stairs, eyes lowered, body still. His bag hung heavy on his back, toys clinking softly as they moved. He didn't say anything. He didn't need to.

But his mother stepped close, not pushing, just placing a hand lightly on his shoulder. "*Just for a little while, anak,*" she whispered. "*You'll like the window.*"

Sion gave a slow nod and followed the hallway, climbing each step like he was counting them. When they reached the top, his mum opened the door gently. The room was small but lovely, simple bed, clean sheets, a window that overlooked the neighbour's garden. It was enough.

He walked in and dropped his bag by the corner.

Then he took off his jumper.

It was warm inside, and maybe he forgot. Or maybe he didn't care. The long-sleeved shirt underneath rose slightly as he pulled the jumper over his head, just for a second. That's when his mum saw them, on his arm. Faint lines. Pale and thin. But not old. Not accidental.

She froze, holding his jumper in her hands.

He hadn't noticed. He was already reaching for his iPad, sitting cross-legged on the bed, focused.

Her mouth opened but nothing came out. The door creaked slightly behind her.

Then someone called from downstairs, *"Coffee's ready!"*

Sion looked up. Just briefly.

His mum quickly handed him the jumper. "Here," she said, gently. *"If you get cold."*

He nodded and placed it beside him.

Later, she would sit at the bottom of the stairs and pretend to read scripture with the others. But she wouldn't hear the words. All she could think about was those lines of scars along his arms. Where they came from. What they meant. And how long they had been there without her knowing.

Downstairs, the house was full.

It was one of those homes that always smelled warm, rice just finished cooking, garlic softened in the pan, something sweet cooling in the corner. There was laughter in the kitchen and singing from the hallway. People from Cardiff, Swansea, and Torbay had come together. Folding chairs were pulled out of closets. Plates clinked. Someone handed out sheets for praise and worship.

The leaders from Bristol were kind and welcoming, and everyone had made space for the parents. But still, they felt slightly out of place. Not for lack of kindness, just difference. Not towards the hosts but for the burden that they have been carrying. As always, Sion's mother kept glancing at the stairs.

"*Should we check on him?*" she whispered once.

"*He's okay,*" said his father, not looking up from his cup. "*He has his iPad.*"

There was a talk that night. Someone shared a testimony, raw and honest, and the room fell quiet. Then they began singing again. Hands were raised. People wept softly. It was that kind of night.

But upstairs, Sion heard none of it.

He sat curled by the bed, half-blanketed in moonlight leaking through the small window. His iPad glowed beside him, but he wasn't drawing. His eyes were open, but far off. That blank stare again, the kind his parents had grown used to. A look that wasn't really empty, but full of something else entirely.

The room was quiet, except for the occasional murmur from downstairs.

Then, slowly, the shadows in the room thickened, not dark in a frightening way, but soft, like mist coming in through the walls. The air didn't grow cold. If anything, it became still. Gentle. Expectant.

And then he saw her.

A girl in a red coat stood by the far wall, not more than ten years old. She had dark hair tied back in a ribbon, shoes slightly scuffed, and hands tucked into her pockets. She looked like someone who had walked a long way.

She didn't say hello. Just tilted her head and studied him quietly.

Sion didn't speak. He never spoke in these moments.

"I thought you might be here," she said softly. *"You've been listening."*

He blinked.

"They don't know you see them," she continued. *"They only see what they expect."*

There was a flicker of sadness in her voice, but also peace. Like she wasn't surprised by anything anymore.

"I lost something," she said. *"But I don't remember what it was. Only how it felt."*

Sion nodded slightly, barely more than a breath.

She took a step closer, but not too close.

"You'll remember for me, won't you?" she asked. *"That's why you came."*

Then, just like mist in the morning, she faded. No flash. No vanishing act. Just… gone.

He remained still for some time.

Then slowly reached for his iPad.

They drove back home in silence that night.

PipSqueak had curled himself on Sion's pillow on that night, his fur gently rising and falling against the boy's arm. He hadn't moved for hours, not even when Sion twitched in his sleep, the way he always did after one of the dreams.

By morning, the cat was still there, eyes half-lidded, watching as Sion stirred. The iPad lit up. And the drawing began.

Later that day, his mother found the sketch, left open on the screen while he fell asleep on the desk of the fourth room.

A girl. Red coat. Black ribbon. Pale, patient face.

She stared at it for a long time.

And then she sat down, as if her knees had forgotten how to stand.

Because she knew that face.

She had worn that coat.

Once.

She didn't tell anyone, not yet.

She just sat there beside him as he slept, brushing the hair from his forehead, her eyes fixed on the lines he'd drawn. It was impossible. And yet, there she was. Not imagined, not made up. Her, from another time.

And she wondered, not for the first time, how much her son really saw. How far back he wandered when no one was watching. And what it was that had started calling him there.

Chapter 7

The First Time He Changed Something

The bulb above the sink had been flickering for days.

It buzzed softly whenever the tap ran. A nervous hum that filled the kitchen like a whisper with nowhere to go. Sion's father crouched beneath the sink, fiddling with a wrench, muttering to himself about the leak that had returned again. Tools clinked in the cupboard beside him. The floor was damp. A faint smell of mildew clung to the air.

In the lounge, Sion's mother sat cross-legged on the floor, folding a mound of clothes that had somehow grown since that morning. She always folded on the floor, not the couch, something about the stretch in her back, the old habit of hard floors from childhood. The TV was on low, more for company than attention. A Filipino soap replayed in soft, tragic tones. No one watched it.

Sion was by the hallway, standing in the space where light from both rooms met and blurred. He hadn't spoken all evening. Not unusual. But something about him was... alert. Awake, in a different way.

He watched his mother. Watched her hands fold a shirt, pause slightly, then fold again.

She didn't look up when she said, *"You hungry, anak?"*

No reply. Just the sound of a slow breath.

And then a whisper.

Not a sentence. Not even a clear word. Just a name. "*Selya.*"

His mother froze. Her fingers stopped moving. The shirt she was folding slipped from her lap.

She turned her head slowly, eyes narrowing. *"What did you say?"*

But Sion was already walking away, feet silent on the wood floor, disappearing into the hallway like a shadow melting into dusk.

She sat there for a while. The word didn't mean anything to her. Not right away. But it echoed strangely. Not in her ears but in her chest. A sort of hollow tug, like remembering something you'd never known.

The next day started like any other.

Morning packed itself into sandwiches, car keys, and a mild argument about the laundry. Sion's father left for a client meeting. His mother headed to the hospital for her shift, just a few hours, covering for someone else. Sion didn't say goodbye. He rarely did.

She arrived early, clipped on her ID, and walked straight into the ward's break room to make herself a cup of coffee. There was a shelf above the kettle. She'd always hatcd that shelf, too loose, badly fixed years ago, and never addressed. She reminded herself again to ask maintenance. She stood under it now, reaching for the sugar tin.

And the shelf fell.

A sharp crack, a sound that shouldn't have been there, and she flinched back, just enough, just in time. The wooden plank missed her shoulder by an inch, scattering mugs and a framed staff photo across the linoleum. Shards flew. A cup shattered at her feet.

No one else was in the room. No one saw it.

But she stood there, heart pounding. In the silence that followed, she heard it again in her mind.

"Selya."

She didn't know what it meant. But somehow, she knew it had meant *this*.

That night, Sion sat in the window room.

The brook outside was restless, its gentle noise carried through the glass, like breathing. His iPad was on his lap, screen still. One hand lay idle on the cushion, the other hovering above a drawing.

It was half-finished. A hallway. A woman. A shadow falling. No colour. Just pencil lines shaped like memory.

He touched the screen.

And the image disappeared.

It didn't fade. It *evaporated* as if it had never been drawn, never thought of, never known.

Sion blinked.

There were other drawings stored on the device. He checked them. Still there. Unchanged.

But this one, this particular sketch, was gone.

He didn't move. He didn't whisper.

He just looked at his hand. Then turned it over.

Something had shifted. Something he hadn't tried to control, but had somehow touched.

He hadn't told anyone. Hadn't said anything except that one name.

But something had listened.

Something had obeyed.

And in the quiet, with the brook murmuring behind the glass, Sion whispered, not to anyone in the room, not even to himself, but to the space just beyond the silence:

"If I take it away... where does it go?"

CHAPTER 8
The Brightness That Blinds

It was November, just days before Advent, when the snow came early. Sharp and sudden, like a warning whispered into the sky.

Sion's family had travelled up north the night before, eight hours of motorway and fog, up into Consett, County Durham. They were there for a Christian retreat, the kind his attends a few times a year. A weekend of prayer, talks, praise. His father had planned the music. His mother packed the thermos. They arrived near midnight at Niwreg's house—a leader in the community, known for his bear-like laugh and creased shirts that always smelled of peppermint.

There was warmth in the house. Soft laughter. The way voices softened around tea. The grown-ups spoke in Taglish and quiet joy. Sion didn't speak much, he never did—but he sat near the edge of the sofa where he could see the firelight flicker against the bookshelves. He liked how the shadows moved without hurrying.

By six the next morning, mugs of coffee steamed on the kitchen counter. Sion's father checked his phone and frowned. A weather warning blinked at the top of the screen: Severe snow. Travel with caution. They were only

thirty minutes from the retreat centre. No one wanted to cancel.

Three cars travelled together in a quiet convoy. Sion's family was in the middle, following the tail-lights of the first vehicle and holding just enough distance from the third. Niwreg's car led the way. Sion's father gripped the wheel tighter than usual.

Five minutes into the journey, the first flakes fell, light, scattered, playful.

By minute ten, they weren't playful anymore.

It came fast. Blinding. Everything white. The kind of snow that didn't fall gently, it rushed in, covered, consumed. The trees blurred. The hedges vanished. Even the road ahead, swallowed.

Only the brake lights of the car in front remained visible—two red dots blinking through a world turned silver. The tarmac faded. Tyre marks appeared, then disappeared just as fast.

Sion sat in his usual spot, behind the passenger seat, left side of the car. His window framed the verge: fences, occasional trees, a sky that looked scraped raw. He liked it that way. He could see the world pass and still feel hidden.

He watched his father through the gap in the headrest. Watched his hands grip the steering wheel. One glance into the rear-view mirror showed the faint glow of the third car but only for a moment. Then it, too, dissolved into the brightness.

The satnav spoke: *"Take the second exit at the roundabout."*

But the lead car didn't.

It veered right, taking the third. Narrower. Tighter. Less cleared.

Sion's father hesitated, then followed.

He didn't want to lose them.

The road narrowed again. Now they were in a residential area, terraced houses, identical and tight together. Parked cars lined the left side, snug against the kerb. On the right, empty space. No double parking allowed, maybe. Or maybe everyone there just kept to themselves.

Then, up ahead, Niweg's car skidded.

Not dramatically. Just a swerve. A quick adjustment. The driver corrected it.

But that was enough.

Sion's father braked.

Too late.

The tyres responded slowly, then not at all. They slid. Left. Then right. The car twisted.

Sion's mother gasped and reached for the dashboard.

Sion didn't scream. He didn't even close his eyes. He stared through the side window, watching the parked cars blur past. They were spinning now. Slow but certain. The road dropped ever so slightly, and gravity pulled them the rest of the way.

The first car had gone.

The third was gone.

They were alone.

And then—

Impact.

Not a crunch. Not a shatter.

Just a deep, dull thud.

But they hadn't hit a car.

It felt… different.

The vehicle jolted, bounced once on its shocks, and tilted sharply to the left. They almost tipped. Almost.

Then, stillness.

A breath held.

Then released.

Sion blinked.

They were facing sideways in the road, just inches from a row of parked cars. No visible damage. No airbags. The engine still on, dazed but alive.

His father stared ahead, knuckles white on the wheel.

"*I thought we hit something*," he said, almost to himself. "*I thought*"

He turned to check on his son.

And froze.

Sion wasn't in his seat.

His seatbelt was unfastened.

He was now on the right side of the car, belt securely clicked in place.

He hadn't moved. His eyes were wide open.

His expression calm.

Still.

His mother turned, confused. "*Did he climb over?*"

They both knew he hadn't. There wasn't time. No noise. No motion. And yet he'd been moved.

His father whispered a prayer he didn't remember learning. His mother already grabbed the rosary beds on her hand.

Outside, snow fell heavier.

Inside, everything glowed too white. Like the light itself had weight.

And somewhere in that brightness, something had passed through.

Something that caught them. Held them. Moved Sion to safety without waking him. Something that stopped them from colliding.

Something that was already gone.

They sat there for minutes.

Eventually, the wipers started again. The snow blurred and ran. The lead car had disappeared into the white. The third car never reappeared.

They drove slowly, inching along. The road twisted, the slope steepened. The wheels slipped often. More than once, they stopped and waited, hoping someone else would appear.

No one did.

They were alone now. The snow erased everything.

At one point, his father parked the car and stepped out, shoes crunching the ice. No boots. They were not prepared for this. He looked around. No landmarks. No people. No signal. Just rows of blank white and houses hiding behind windows.

He climbed back in and turned the wheel gently.

"We'll try a bit further," he said.

Every few metres, the tyres fought the road.

Once, they spun halfway again.

But the car kept upright.

Eventually, the road opened into a clearer stretch. A sign, barely visible, pointed to the retreat venue. They were close.

Too close to give up now.

At the edge of the estate, the road stopped being road. The snow covered it entirely. They left the car at the bottom of the hill and walked the rest of the way.

Their boots sank ankle-deep.

Sion didn't complain.

He walked without effort, as if the path had been made for him.

At the top of the slope, the retreat house waited. Lights on. Doors open. Warmth rising from the chimney.

Inside, people sang.

Outside, the world was white.

Later that night, when the car was checked, there were no dents. No scrapes. Nothing to mark what they'd hit.

Nothing at all.

But Sion knew.

Whatever had been in that brightness, it hadn't come to harm.

It had come to protect.

And before the light vanished…

it had whispered one thing to him, so soft even the snow couldn't hear:

"Not today."

CHAPTER 9
The Night Garden

It was 3:30 in the cold, wintery November morning.

The street outside their house was still, barely lit by a single working lamp that flickered like it had a secret to tell. All the other lights along the road had gone dark months ago. The council never fixed them.

Sion opened the front door slowly, pressing his fingers against the stiff brass latch so it wouldn't click. He moved with practiced silence, each step already mapped in his head.

His mother was on night shift. His father was asleep upstairs, curled on his side like always, wrapped in the grey blanket he never changed. Sion knew the rhythm of his father's sleep. Knew he wouldn't wake.

He also knew where every CCTV was pointed. One above the main door. One above the porch. The other by the shed, and a dozen more spread in and outside of the house. He stepped through their blind spots like shadows slipping between light. Then he crossed the cul-de-sac and ducked into the tall bushes at the edge of the trees.

No one saw him.

The pavement turned into gravel. The gravel turned into dirt. It had rained a few days ago and the path was slick underfoot. He nearly slipped twice but didn't fall. His thin trainers soaked through quickly, but he didn't care.

He moved through the dark with the calm of someone who had already seen where he needed to go.

The forest wasn't far—just behind the housing estate, past the broken fence where kids used to sneak out to smoke. But Sion went deeper. Past the old bike frame rusting near the path. Past the graffitied bench no one sat on anymore.

The trees closed in.

It wasn't a thick forest. But at this hour, with no torch and only the faint light of the moon behind clouds, it might as well have been a thousand miles wide. The air here had a different kind of silence. Not empty—but full of watching things.

And in the middle of it, where the trees thinned into a natural clearing, was what he called the garden.

It wasn't a real garden. Not with neat hedges or planted rows.

But to Sion, it felt alive.

The grass grew thick and strange here, even in November. The air was colder but moved gently, as if stirred by breath. And the earth had that soft give under his feet, the kind that said something was buried deep beneath.

He stepped into the clearing.

Time… shifted.

Seconds stretched longer than they should. Sounds folded in on themselves. And the moonlight—when it finally broke through the bare trees—bent strangely across the clearing, like it had passed through water first.

He crouched by a patch of exposed soil, right at the base of a crooked tree whose bark peeled like burnt paper.

His fingers dug without hesitation. The earth was cold, but loose.

And then he found it.

A feather. Black. Not glossy, not oily like a crow's. This one looked like it had no colour at all, only the memory of darkness. It was long and unnaturally smooth, heavier than any feather ought to be. When his skin touched it, a soft vibration pulsed in his fingers, like holding something that was still slightly alive.

He didn't flinch.

Just stared.

Then he slipped it into the inside pocket of his jacket and stood up.

No drawing. No whisper. No sound.

He walked home the way he came, carefully. The wind had picked up a little. The trees sighed. And somewhere, not far off, a fox screamed once into the dark.

He stepped through the blind spots again. Quietly closed the front door. His socks left little wet trails on the floor, but he wiped them away with his sleeve. Then he climbed the stairs two at a time and disappeared into his room.

He didn't draw that night. He didn't sleep either. Not right away.

He opened the tin box in the back of his cupboard— where old coins, memory sticks, and folded paper lived in quiet company. He placed the feather inside and shut it gently.

The feather pulsed once, faintly, from inside the tin.

And just before he drifted off—eyes wide open, facing the ceiling, he felt it: Not a fear. But a presence.

Something watching. Something waiting. Just beyond the edges of what could be seen.

And as he touched the feather again, barely breathing, he whispered into the soil—

"If this is where they fall… where do they fly from?"

CHAPTER 10

The Whispers Are Not His Own

At first, they thought it was the wind.

Just a faint rustle. A shift in the air. His mum would pass his bedroom door in the night and pause, listening. Sometimes she'd open it slowly, expecting silence, and find him lying still under the blanket, arms folded, face turned to the wall. Nothing out of place. Nothing wrong.

But sometimes… he whispered.

It was barely a sound. Like breath brushing across glass. A murmur that seemed to echo, even when the room was quiet. His lips would move, but the words weren't his. Not the way he usually spoke. Not soft, shy, or halting like his daytime voice.

These whispers had shape. Rhythm. Sometimes quick and clipped, sometimes slow like the dragging of a heavy chain.

One night, his mother stood just outside his door. It was past 2am. She hadn't meant to stay up so late, but the laundry had piled again, and her back was aching from the shift. She reached for the hallway light switch, then froze.

Sion was speaking.

Not loud. Not waking.

Whispering.

At first, it sounded like gibberish. But the longer she listened, the more she realised, it wasn't nonsense. It was language. Several, in fact. Some sounded like old Tagalog, the kind spoken by her grandfather in the provinces of Zamboanga. One whisper had the lilting sharpness of German. Another, slow and trembling, repeated something in a voice that didn't sound like a child at all.

She stepped into the room.

Sion didn't move.

His eyes were closed, but his mouth kept forming words. Pausing, continuing. Sometimes the tone changed, like someone else was speaking through him. Then another. And another. Each voice carried something heavy. Pleading. Regretful. Some whispered names. Others wept.

She backed out slowly, heart in her throat, and didn't sleep the rest of the night.

The next day, she told her husband. He laughed it off at first. *"He probably heard something online. One of those creepy YouTube videos,"* he said.

But when it happened again, he recorded it.

It was a Wednesday. The weather had turned, and the pipes in the house made strange noises all evening. At 3:12am, the whispers began. They were louder this time. Sion was on his back, hands curled into the blanket, lips moving fast. His father pressed record on his phone and held it steady for nearly ten minutes.

When he played it back the next morning, the house fell quiet.

The voices were clear. A woman's voice, broken and cracking, whispered the same sentence three times. Then a child sobbed something in a dialect they didn't recognise.

After that, the line went silent, until a soft humming tune emerged. A lullaby. Familiar, but warped.

Sion had never heard it before. At least, not in this lifetime.

Later that week, the recording was accidentally played aloud when Sion entered the kitchen. He stopped. His body tensed. Then, without a word, he turned and left the room. His mother found him an hour later, curled in the corner of the hallway, arms wrapped tightly around his knees.

He hadn't drawn all day.

That night, he did.

He sketched quickly. Feverishly. As if the pencil couldn't keep up. He didn't draw a face or a monster. He drew a name. Over and over again. In thick, overlapping lines. The name *Isabel*. Then beneath it, in smaller handwriting, *age nine*. At the bottom of the page, just one line:

"Buried near the old church. No one looked."

When his mother found the drawing the next morning, she stared at it for a long time. She didn't recognise the name. But something about it chilled her. The handwriting wasn't even like Sion's usual strokes, it was tight, jagged, urgent.

That afternoon, she Googled it. Isabel. Nine years old. Missing since 1978. Last seen near a small chapel just two towns over. Never found.

She sat down on the kitchen floor, phone in her hand, drawing in the other.

And for the first time, she wondered if her son's whispers were not dreams at all.

That night, Sion whispered again.

But this time, one of the voices paused. And whispered *her* name.

And from somewhere in the dark, Sion—still fast asleep—smiled faintly.

There was another time.

More recent. Quieter, in a different way.

His father had stopped sleeping in the master bedroom. He now kept to the smaller room at the end of the hall, the one with the creaky floor and no curtains. No one spoke about it, not even in passing. But Sion noticed. He always noticed.

His mum still cooked the same meals. Still packed lunchboxes. Still asked, *"Have you brushed your teeth?"* like nothing had changed. But sometimes, after dishes were done and the house had gone dim, he'd hear it.

A small sound. Careful. Tucked into the pillow.

Crying.

It didn't come in sobs. Not like movies. It was the sort of crying that stayed beneath the breath. A shudder of lungs. A sound that didn't want to be heard, but needed to get out.

She cried most often around 1:00 in the morning. Sion kept track. Not with a clock, but by the feel of it. A shift in the house. The way the hallway air cooled. The way the tap in the kitchen let out a single drop just before it began.

He sat on the floor of his room, drawing nothing. Just holding the pencil.

Then he stood.

Walked to the corner where the shadows were thicker. Sat again. Knees up, arms around them. Head resting to the side.

And slowly, he reached under his sleeve.

This time, he didn't hesitate. His fingers found the inside of his arm, already lined with faded echoes. He pinched. Hard. Until his breath caught in his throat and the heat spread up his skin like fire licking through ice.

Her pain moved. He felt it.

Her disappointment. Her weariness. Her quiet mourning for something she couldn't fix. All of it flowed like smoke into his chest. It stung behind his ribs. It pulsed in his jaw. His eyes filled, but he didn't cry.

He just held it.

Then, in the next room over, something changed.

He heard movement. A light click. The sound of slippers on the wood floor. Then the fridge door.

She was downstairs now.

Opening the bread bin. Clinking two plates together.

Preparing a snack.

Nothing fancy. Just two slices of pandesal, warmed in the pan. She laid them out with butter, carefully. Like she had before. Before everything cracked.

Then she carried the plate to the small room at the end of the hall. She didn't knock. Just opened the door, stepped in, and said, "*Nagugutom ka ba*?" Are you hungry?

Sion didn't hear what his father said. Only that the door stayed open a little longer this time.

He smiled softly in the dark.

Not proud. Not triumphant.

Just… relieved.

The pain had passed. For now.

He looked at his arm. The pinch had broken skin again. A bead of red welled to the surface, blooming like a small offering.

He wiped it away gently and pulled the sleeve back down.

The voices would return later.

But for now the house was still.

And someone had just said thank you with warm bread.

Later that night, Sion sat by the window again, knees to chest, the blanket wrapped around him like a hush. His arm ached, but it was a quiet kind of pain, something settled, like the air after rain.

He didn't need words to explain what happened.

He just knew.

Sometimes, love doesn't come with answers or apologies. Sometimes, it's just a plate of warm bread offered in silence. And sometimes, it takes someone else's pain to make space for that moment to exist.

He whispered into the glass, not to be heard, but to remember:

"If I must carry it, let it make room for something good."

And with that, the night settled again. The house breathed softly. And the boy who never quite belonged to time closed his eyes, just for a while.

CHAPTER 11

When the Past Pulls You In

It was a Saturday.

No appointments. No prayer meetings. Just a slow, grey morning, damp with the kind of rain that never falls properly, just hangs in the air like breath.

Sion didn't come down for breakfast.

At first, his mother thought he was just tired. He'd been quieter than usual the night before, hadn't touched his drawing or his iPad, only sat curled in the corner of the sofa with a blanket around his shoulders.

But when it neared midday and still no movement from upstairs, she climbed the steps with gentle feet and pushed open his door.

He was there. Lying on his side. Breathing.

But still.

Eyes closed, not in rest—but in retreat. His skin looked cold. His lips, slightly parted, as if he'd meant to whisper but forgot the words. One hand was tucked under his chest. The other curled loosely by his face.

She called his name once.

Then again, louder.

No response.

She touched his shoulder. Warm, but unreactive.

Downstairs, his father said he was probably just exhausted, or faking sleep. But something in his mother's face said otherwise. She sat by his bed for hours, fingers brushing through his hair, murmuring things in Tagalog that didn't quite reach him.

Because Sion wasn't there.

Not really.

He'd been pulled somewhere else.

It began in the usual way, just a dull weight behind his ribs, then a strange hum under his skin. But this time, it didn't pass. It deepened. Thickened. Like a current pulling at his ankles. He felt the world lean sideways, and before he could draw or whisper or blink, he was gone.

The room around him dissolved like chalk in water.

Then came the cold.

Not the cold of winter or wind, but the still cold of an old stone wall. Dust in the air. Silence so deep it rang in his ears. He stood barefoot on wooden floorboards, pale light slicing through slats in a boarded window. The walls were high and cracked. In the far corner, a metal basin. A chair. A single shoe.

It wasn't his time. That much he knew.

This place had its own air, its own echo. And it remembered everything.

A girl's name scratched faintly into the wooden beam. A worn teddy half hidden beneath the bedframe. Scraps of paper tucked behind loose plaster, drawings, maybe, though he didn't dare touch them.

Sion stood there, still, quiet, like he belonged to the dust.

In that moment, he didn't feel afraid.

Just… tethered. Like a thread of himself had been here before.

Then—footsteps.

Heavy. Coming closer.

But no one appeared.

Just the sound, circling the edge of the space, never entering.

Then, a breath, soft and warm against his cheek.

He turned.

No one.

Only a flicker. A girl, just for a second, sitting on the edge of the bed. Looking at her hands. Then gone.

And Sion felt it, not panic, but an urgency. A need to remember something that wasn't his. A memory reaching for him, hoping he'd carry it back.

A sharp weight filled his chest. Sadness that had no shape, only a single wish.

Let me go.

When he woke, it was dark.

His skin was cold. His lips dry.

He sat up slowly, heartbeat out of rhythm with the room.

The light outside had changed. Rain still pressed against the window like it never stopped.

He pulled the blanket closer. Still dazed. Still halfthere.

And with his finger, slow and unsure, he began to write on the wall.

Not with ink. Not with blood.

Just his finger.

The pressure of it left faint trails in the dust near the windowpane, just visible in the gloom.

First, the word:

SUICIDE

All capitals. Uneven. Pressed hard. Large enough to take over half the wall.

Then smaller words began to form underneath, scattered like broken thoughts.

It's better this way. I'm not meant to stay.

Let me go. I don't want to feel anymore.

Please don't make me stay. I want the pain to stop.

They weren't his words. He knew that. He didn't even think them—he just carried them. They moved through him like a current, a voice desperate to be heard through someone else's body.

They belonged to the girl in the room. Her pain, raw and unspoken, had needed somewhere to go.

And it had found him.

When his mother finally came back up, thinking he might've finally stirred, she opened the door gently.

What she saw pulled the air out of her lungs.

Her son, sitting quietly in bed, pale and silent. And behind him, across the wall: the word.

SUICIDE in huge, brutal strokes.

The smaller words scattered like a whispering storm around it.

She froze.

Everything inside her dropped.

Then she ran to him, arms around his shoulders, voice trembling.

"Oh my God, anak. Anak—no, no, no…"

Sion didn't move away.

He just rested his head against her chest and whispered one thing, soft enough to almost vanish:

"Not me."

She held him tighter.

The next day, he drew.

Not a creature. Not a monster.

But the room.

Every crack in the wall. The slats. The girl on the bed.

He didn't even need to look at the paper, his hands knew where the lines belonged.

He didn't speak about it.

He didn't need to.

Some feelings aren't meant to be understood. Only carried, until they can rest somewhere else.

CHAPTER 12

Creatures That Feed On Silence

It started with a drawing.

A new one. Unfinished.

A figure crouched beneath a table. Limbs thin and wiry, wrapped around themselves like thread wound too tight. No face—just a hollow swirl where the head should be. Around the figure were strands, long and dark, slithering from its back, wrapping around chairs, walls, doorframes. Like vines. Or veins.

The room in the drawing looked familiar. Too familiar.

It was his classroom.

Sion didn't remember starting the drawing, but it was there—on his iPad when he woke. The lines were smooth, careful. Not rushed like most sketches made in the haze of night. This one had purpose. Focus.

He stared at it for a long while, fingers hovering over the screen.

That morning, school felt heavier. Not louder, not brighter—just... thick. Like the air was made of water and everyone was wading through it without knowing. Sion's teacher, Mr Henson, didn't smile when he greeted the class. He didn't correct the talkative boys at the back. He barely looked up when Callum kicked someone's chair.

Sion noticed something else, too.

A shape. Subtle. Lurking.

Wrapped around Mr Henson's shoulders, coiled tight like a scarf made of shadow. No one else reacted. But Sion's eyes fixed on it.

It wasn't fully formed, not like the creatures he drew after feeling people's pain. This one pulsed gently. Feeding. Its skin was translucent, like it hadn't quite made it through yet.

It was feeding on silence.

Not just any silence—the kind that builds up when people bury too much. The kind that lives in long-held secrets and things left unsaid. And Mr Henson… he was full of them. Quiet regret in the way he slouched his shoulders. Guilt in the way he avoided the window. A face that used to smile, now just going through the motions.

At lunch, Sion sat in his usual spot, away from the others.

He didn't eat much.

He sketched again, fast, like he couldn't hold the lines in any longer. The creature on Mr Henson's shoulders took shape. Its limbs stretched out now, latching onto desks, pens, notebooks. It fed not with its mouth, but by wrapping itself tighter each time something was left unsaid.

Sion could feel it… feeding.

And that night, it happened again.

He felt the pull.

Not from a memory, but from a moment still happening. His head throbbed. His fingers trembled. He saw

Mr Henson alone in his flat, still in his tie, sitting at the edge of the bed, staring at the floor like he'd forgotten how to sleep. There was a letter. Not opened. Not touched. And silence. Crushing silence.

Sion couldn't watch anymore.

He pinched his arm. Hard.

And the creature in the sketch twitched.

He felt it surge through him. The weight of words Mr Henson had never said. The pain of losing someone and never telling them it hurt. Regret wrapped around the spine. It clawed at Sion's ribs, then quieted, like something settling into him.

He curled up in bed, whispering not words, but breaths.

And when he finally drifted into sleep, his mind burned with the image of vines, black, stretching, and a man slowly lifting his head for the first time in weeks.

The next morning at school, Mr Henson spoke more. Not much. But he smiled, slightly, when someone got an answer right. He even wrote something on the board that made half the class laugh.

But Sion knew the creature wasn't fully gone. Not yet.

Because silence doesn't break all at once. It thins. It frays. And then one day, it's gone.

Some people scream and you hear them right away. But others... they sink into silence so deep, you only hear them if you're willing to listen where no one else is listening.

CHAPTER 13
The Room With No Time

There was a door in their attic. Not hidden exactly, just forgotten. Behind storage boxes and Christmas tinsel and the plastic tree that had lost most of its needles.

Sion didn't know why he noticed it that night. Only that he did.

He'd gone up for a blanket. That's what he told himself. The air had been cold, and the hallway light buzzed overhead like something half-awake. He moved quietly, socks sliding on the floorboards, past the second bedroom where his father used to sleep when he was suffering from depression.

The attic ladder groaned when he pulled it down. No one stirred.

He climbed slowly, each rung familiar from the dozens of times he'd been up there with his mum, fetching old clothes or sorting boxes for donation. But this time he didn't stop at the shelves. He turned left, past the suitcases. And that's when he saw it.

A narrow door. Unpainted. Warped slightly at the bottom.

He didn't remember it being there.

His hand reached out before he could think about it. The handle was cool, dry. He turned it.

The hinges gave way without sound.

Inside, nothing at first. Just dust. The stale breath of long-forgotten things. But then the air changed. Sion stepped in, and the room swallowed sound.

Utter quiet.

Not peaceful quiet but strange. Thick. Like stepping underwater.

The space wasn't big. Just wide enough for him to stand and turn. No windows. No light bulb. But he could see. Everything inside glowed faintly, like moonlight from nowhere.

Old papers. Broken toys. One of his mum's high heels missing the buckle. Sets of old keys. His mother always losing keys. But there was something else, something beneath it all.

A pull.

Time didn't feel right in here.

He crouched in the corner where the wall met the floor and ran his fingers along the wooden beam. It hummed. Gently. Like touching the surface of a memory.

And then…images.

Not from now. Not from him.

A boy in the 70s, scratching words into the wood with a house key. A teenage girl lying on the floor, crying without sound. A man counting coins, over and over, lips moving in prayer. All of them in the same space. All of them unaware of each other. But their moments… overlapped.

Sion blinked.

It was like the walls held their time. Trapped it. Not to imprison, but to remember.

He found a pile of yellowed paper tucked behind an old suitcase. Crayon drawings, shaky handwriting. None of it his, but some of the pictures were familiar. A shadow with no face. A door with eyes. A girl with a red coat.

His breath caught.

He sat down and pulled out his iPad.

Not to draw, but to listen.

The whispers came slowly at first. Not like the ones that spilled from his mouth in sleep. These were quieter. Etched into the grain of the floorboards. Threaded into the dust. He didn't hear them with his ears. He felt them.

A sorrow from 1961. A secret from 1985. Regrets older than his father. Voices without sound, stitched into the bones of the house.

He opened his small sketch journal, the one he kept hidden from everyone.

And wrote:

"There's something kind here. But it remembers too much."

Then he began to draw. Not creatures this time. Not pain.

He drew *time*.

Moments blurred together. Hands reaching across years. Eyes watching from inside old photographs. A clock melting into tree roots. He drew until the quiet felt full again.

He stayed in that room for hours. But when he stepped out, it had only been ten minutes.

His fingers were dusty. His lips dry. His head light.

But inside, something pulsed.

Not like before. Not pain. Not burden.

This was something else.

A deep sense of *place*. Like he had stepped into the spine of the world.

That night, Sion slept.

Not in bed, but in the attic room.

And when he woke, his drawings had changed again.

Not darker. Not lighter.

Just… deeper.

Time doesn't always move forward. Sometimes, it waits. Sometimes, it folds. And sometimes, if you listen closely, it speaks back.

CHAPTER 14
The Day He Vanished

At first, they thought he was just sleeping in.

It was a Sunday. The sky over Cardiff was heavy with clouds, the kind that threatened rain but couldn't be bothered to start. The house was still. His mum had brewed coffee, his father had gone to buy bread. The usual.

But by noon, Sion still hadn't come down.

No sound of tapping. No footsteps. No whispered greetings. Nothing.

His mother knocked lightly on his door.

No answer.

She turned the handle and stepped inside.

There he was, on the bed, lying on his side, facing the wall. Curled inwards like he'd only just drifted off. His chest rose and fell. His mouth slightly open. Eyes shut.

But something was off.

His fingers were too still. His hair didn't twitch with breath. Even in sleep, Sion usually moved, twitched a toe, shifted his knee, mumbled soft words. But not this time. He didn't stir.

She whispered, "*Anak?*"

No response.

She touched his arm. Warm. Breathing. But gone.

She called his name louder. Still nothing.

"*No. Not again.*" She exclaimed.

By the time his father returned, she was already on the phone with NHS 111, pacing the kitchen with shaking hands.

They checked everything, his pulse, his breathing, his temperature. All normal. He just… wouldn't wake.

They took him to A&E.

The nurse tried to lift his eyelids. The boy didn't flinch. A neurologist was paged. Then another. Blood tests. Scans. A CT. Everything showed a healthy, resting brain.

But Sion wasn't there.

Not really.

He was somewhere else.

It had started the night before. Quietly. Like most things with him.

He'd been drawing in the attic room again. Pages scattered around him like fallen leaves. Faces and shadows. Words that didn't belong to him. Symbols he didn't understand but felt compelled to sketch. The hum in the walls had grown stronger, low and constant, like the earth humming in sleep.

Then it happened.

A blink.

One moment, Sion was there, kneeling on the attic floor, pencil in hand.

The next…

He was on a different street. One that hadn't existed in decades.

Brick buildings loomed overhead, chipped and water-stained. A red post-box stood crooked near a kerb. The sky was darker, like someone had turned the colour down.

And everything smelled faintly of coal smoke.

He walked. Or thought he did. The ground beneath him didn't feel right. Too soft. Too slow. Every step felt like it was being remembered, not taken.

Children ran past him, thin arms, muddy boots, laughter that echoed as if it came from the bottom of a well.

A man with soot on his face tipped his cap at someone who no longer stood there.

Sion turned a corner and saw her.

The girl with the red coat.

Older now. Maybe fourteen. Her hair longer. Her mouth hard.

She stood near a church gate, staring at something just out of view.

He tried to call her name—though he wasn't sure he ever knew it.

But his voice didn't work here.

Only his presence did.

She turned. Eyes wide, like she'd felt him.

Then, without speaking, she stepped back, into a shadow that split across the stone wall.

And vanished.

Sion felt it then.

A pull.

Not a physical one. But deep. Through his ribs. His spine.

Like the world had tried to swallow him whole.

Back in the hospital, his mother was holding his hand. Whispering prayers. Bits of rosary. Her fingers trembled.

The doctors had no answers. They used words like *trauma-triggered shutdown, unexplained coma.*

But Sion wasn't unconscious.

He was busy.

Not in a dream. Not lost.

Just elsewhere.

And wherever he had gone—he was needed.

I didn't leave my body.

I just followed the ache.

And sometimes, pain is louder than waking.

CHAPTER 15

The Whisper That Shattered Time

It started with breath.

A long, steady inhale.

After two full days of silence, Sion's chest rose, not just the shallow rhythm of a sleeping body, but fuller, with intent. His mother had just stepped out to refill her cup. His father was asleep on the chair beside him, arms crossed over his chest like a shield.

His father's eye bags were now so heavy they looked like they could grow legs, jump off his face, and walk out of the room on their own. He hadn't had proper sleep in years, not since Sion was born. Not really. Even on nights when the house was quiet, he'd stay half-awake, listening for movement, watching the baby monitor long after Sion had outgrown it. His weariness had grown into a habit, etched into the lines of his face, stitched into every sigh.

He stirred now in the chair but didn't wake. His neck bent awkwardly to one side, his mouth slightly open. One hand twitched every now and then, like his body was still trying to catch something it couldn't hold. The blanket someone had draped over him had slipped off hours ago, but he hadn't noticed. Or maybe he didn't care. His sleep was never deep, more like a long blink that never brought rest.

Sion's breath deepened again. Then, slowly, his lips parted.

A whisper slipped out. Not in his usual voice. It was low, almost gritty, as if it had been carried a long way to get here. The air shifted. The light in the room dimmed, not darker, just softer, like everything had taken a step back to listen.

Across the room, a photo frame rattled gently on the shelf.

It fell.

His father jolted awake with a small gasp, his hand flying to his chest. He blinked rapidly, heart thudding, unsure whether the sound had come from the world or his dreams.

He looked at Sion. The boy hadn't moved since.

Still lying there. Eyes shut. Breathing even.

But something had changed.

The father leaned forward slowly, rubbing his temples. His shoulders sagged in the chair as if they were carrying more than just his body. His whole frame looked folded in on itself, like he was always preparing to brace for something. Another silence. Another surprise.

He picked up the fallen frame. It was the family photo from five years ago before things got hard. Before the drawings. Before the whispers. Before the long nights and longer days. They looked happy in the photo. Younger. Like they hadn't learned to flinch yet.

He stared at it for a moment too long. Then set it back upright, face-down this time.

His fingers brushed Sion's hair.

"*Anak*," he said softly, more breath than sound.

Sion didn't answer.

But the room felt... lighter. Not peaceful. But less burdened somehow.

And for a fleeting second, as he looked at his son, still so pale, so quiet, his father's tired heart allowed something close to hope.

Then…

Sion whispered.

One word.

Not mumbled. Not slurred. Spoken.

Clear. Quiet. Carved from the stillness of the room.

It was enough.

The air changed. Subtle. Sharp. Like pressure lifting after a storm. Somewhere in the ward, a bin rolled two inches by itself. The wall clock skipped ahead by a second. And the monitor beside Sion gave a single, confused beep.

His father stirred. Blinked. Looked at his son then leaned in closer.

"*Sion?*" he said softly.

Sion's lips didn't move again. His body remained still.

But the whisper stayed in the air like a note struck too gently to hear but too strong to ignore.

When his mother returned, her eyes lit up. "*Did he speak?*"

His father nodded slowly. "*Just one word.*"

"*What did he say?*"

He opened his mouth to repeat it. But paused.

He couldn't remember.

Not exactly.

But something about it still echoed behind his ribs.

Like he had known it once. In another life.

The next morning, as the doctors prepared another round of scans, something else shifted.

Back home, a photo fell from the shelf in the living room. No wind. No quake. Just a soft clatter against the floorboards.

It landed face-up.

A sepia image. Faded with age. Three boys standing by a canal, their shoes caked in mud. One wore a flat cap too big for his head. One had a scar above his brow.

The third was unmistakable.

Same sharp chin. Same eyebrows pulled slightly inward.

Sion.

But not any version of him his parents had ever seen.

His mother knelt to pick it up, holding it gently by the corner.

"Do you remember this?" she asked.

His father stared. Then frowned.

"We've never owned that photo."

In the attic, the journal Sion kept had a page missing.

Not torn—gone.

Vanished cleanly from the middle of the book. The next page began mid-sentence. His sketches on the previous page bled into nothing. Colours faded. Lines unfinished.

Something had been erased.

Or rewritten.

Later that night, as they stood by his bed once more, watching the way his breath moved evenly under the blanket, his mother reached for her rosary, but stopped midway.

She didn't feel afraid anymore.

Just changed.

Like something in the room had shifted their place in the world. A thread pulled loose and retied, just slightly off-centre.

That single whispered word had done something.

It had bent time, if only for a moment.

When the world forgets, I remember.

When time tries to heal by hiding,

I whisper it back into place.

CHAPTER 16

His Name in Someone Else's Story

It started with a letter. Plain white envelope. No return address. Folded carefully, like the sender meant it to last.

His mother found it among the usual post, council notices, a flyer for a missing cat, and a bill they couldn't afford. The envelope was unmarked except for one word, written in small, looping handwriting:

Sion.

She stared at it for a while before opening it.

Inside:

A single sheet. A single sentence.

"Tell him thank you. I never jumped. I never even went up the stairs."

No name. No signature.

She didn't understand. But Sion, reading over her shoulder, went very still.

He knew who it was from.

It was the girl from the whisper. The one whose pain he'd pulled into himself like smoke through cracked glass. The one who nearly ended everything. He remembered the weight of her grief, the spiral of her thoughts, how loud it had been before it settled in his own bones. He'd carried that silence for weeks, until it became part of his own.

Now she was still here. Still alive. Because of him.

But it didn't stop there.

A week later, at the school gate, a woman touched his mother's arm. *"Excuse me,"* she said, hesitating. *"Is your boy... is his name Sion?"*

His mother nodded, unsure.

The woman's eyes filled. *"I think he saved my son."*

She said he'd changed. Just like that. One day, the boy stopped hiding in cupboards. Stopped trembling when the front door opened. He'd started drawing again. Laughing. He said it was a dream. That a quiet boy found him under the staircase and whispered something into his chest. *"I don't remember the words,"* the boy said. *"But it made the bad thing leave."*

Sion's mother smiled politely, confused. But Sion... he lowered his head. Not in shame. In reverence.

He remembered that night. The pain that clung to the boy's lungs. The shame that curled like smoke around his ribs. He remembered whispering something, words he didn't fully understand but knew would work. And they did.

And then there were more.

A woman who swore she'd seen him once in 1964, as a child in a yellow coat. He was standing at the corner of the road where her brother had died. *"He looked like he didn't belong,"* she said, *"but he smiled at me. I've never forgotten it."*

A man at the train station stopped his father. Said, *"You've got a son, yeah? Little quiet one?"* When Sion's father nodded, wary, the man simply said, *"He helped me once. Don't know how. But I'm still here because of him."* Then he walked away.

It wasn't always dramatic. Sometimes it was small.

A stranger waving across the street. A girl who left a drawing at their door. A text message from an unknown number: *"He was in my dream again. He told me it's not too late."*

The whispers were growing.

Sion's name had become a thread, weaving through stories that weren't his. Memories where he didn't belong—but somehow, had always been.

And it was starting to change him.

He couldn't always tell what was his and what wasn't. Sometimes he'd wake up with words in his head he didn't recognise. Sometimes he'd feel a memory as if it were his own—only to realise it belonged to someone else. He was slipping through the seams of other people's lives.

Even his drawings had started to shift.

They used to be sharp, full of shadow and form, monsters with claws and teeth, born from the pain he absorbed. Now, they were different. Lighter. Some showed moments of peace. A mother hugging her son. A boy letting go of a rope. A girl stepping off a ledge, but up, not down.

The demons weren't gone. Not completely. But some had been... released.

Transferred. Taken.

He didn't always know where they went. But they weren't with those people anymore.

His mother found him sketching one of those scenes, the kind that felt too still to be just imagination. "*Where do you see these things?*" she asked.

He didn't answer. But he looked at her.

And in his eyes, those tired, knowing eyes, was a hint of something that wasn't quite from now.

Maybe I was never meant to stay in just one story, because some people only survive when someone else carries a page for them.

CHAPTER 17

The Last Drawing

It began with silence. But not the usual kind.

This silence was thick, deliberate. Like the world itself had leaned in to watch.

Sion had been in his attic room all night, the one that didn't follow time. His sketchbooks were scattered across the floor, some opened to creatures that had long since vanished from the world, others half-finished, still humming faintly under the pencil strokes. His small tin box sat beside him, the black feather resting on top now, not hidden away.

His iPad lay untouched. Tonight, he didn't need it.

He pulled out a fresh sheet. Larger than he usually used. The kind that took up the whole desk.

His hand hovered for a moment.

Then—he began.

Not fast. Not frantic. But steady. As if the lines already existed and he was just uncovering them.

This was not a drawing of a monster. Nor a place he'd seen in a dream. It wasn't even about someone else's pain.

It was something else entirely.

Shapes began to bloom across the page, roads that curved and split, spirals turning into rivers, doorways carved into trees. Tiny figures appeared next. Some walking, others curled in corners. Some whispering, others being held. And at the centre, like the calm eye of a storm, was a boy. Small, quiet, head slightly tilted.

Sion didn't draw his face.

He didn't need to.

The entire page pulsed with colour—not the harsh hues of anger or sadness he was used to, but warmth. Soft oranges, greys, deep greens. Gentle blue light around the edges, like the hush of dawn before anything moves. It was the first time in a long while he used colour so freely. It bled from the pencils like breath.

And as the last mark was made, the paper shimmered, barely noticeable, but enough.

The image glowed softly in the low light of his room, colours bleeding into one another like water through fabric. It was unlike anything Sion had ever drawn. No creatures. No figures in torment. No whispering shadows.

It was breathing.

This one was… alive.

Lines curled outward from a quiet centre, some thick, some hair-thin, like veins on a leaf. They weren't roads or rivers, not exactly. More like *paths*. Threads of time. Some ran smooth, others tangled and looped back. Here and there, they snapped and stopped short, frayed at the end.

Tiny silhouettes dotted the lines. Human-like but faceless. Some curled inward, clutching invisible grief. Others stood taller, their arms no longer weighted. A woman holding a folded apron. A boy holding nothing. A girl with her head tilted as if listening to something that finally made sense.

The colours told their stories.

At the edges, where pain first took root, reds flared, raw and burning. Closer to the centre, they shifted, softer hues, calmer tones. Bruised blues that gave way to green. Hints of gold near those who had been changed.

There were names, too *faint*, as though written by someone half-asleep. They hovered at the margins, appearing and fading: Callum. Evie. Sofia. Nathaniel. The Girl in Red. Names from moments, from pain carried, from burdens lifted. Some were strangers to the world. All were familiar to Sion.

And in the very centre, at the heart of it all, sat a boy.

Not detailed. No features drawn. Just the outline of someone cross-legged, holding a pencil. Alone. Surrounded by silence that had shape and colour.

It wasn't a drawing meant to be explained. It couldn't be studied or solved. It had to be felt, like grief. Like memory. Like love.

Sion placed it on the floor gently and stepped back. He watched in silence. The colours softened but didn't fade, as if the page itself was still listening, still remembering. It felt alive in a way that needed no movement at all.

Just presence.

And in that moment, for the first time in a long while, he didn't feel like a boy burdened with the world's sorrow.

He felt like a boy who had *loved* the world quietly, completely.

And it had loved him back.

His mum found him sitting in front of it, arms around his knees. He didn't turn when she entered. Didn't speak. Just gestured softly with his chin toward the paper.

She stepped closer.

At first, she didn't understand what she was looking at. But then… she saw it.

The paths. The faces. The almost-living stillness of it. It felt like a map. But not of a place. Not even a moment.

It was a record. A memory trail. Of everything Sion had ever changed.

Every pain he'd carried. Every darkness he'd swallowed. Every soul he'd kept from falling.

And at the edges of the map, names began to appear. Not written by hand, but forming slowly, fading in like mist settling over glass. Familiar names. People who'd once been on the edge.

Some they knew. Most they didn't. But Sion did.

His mother pressed a hand over her mouth. Tears welled, but didn't fall.

The air in the attic shifted. It smelled faintly of smoke and rain. The walls, lined with old drawings, seemed to hold their breath. Even the feather on the desk quivered once, like acknowledging something sacred had just taken place.

This was his last drawing.

He didn't say it. He didn't need to.

Because the room already knew.

Some maps don't lead you to a place. They lead you home— through the lives you helped hold together.

CHAPTER 18

The Choice

The attic was still. Not the quiet of sleep, or the hush of a resting house, but a stillness that asked for nothing. Demanded nothing. Just was.

Sion sat alone in the middle of the floor, his arms around his knees. The map lay before him, glowing faintly in the greying light. The names had stopped appearing now. The paper had gone still. No more shimmer. No more motion. As if the story had finished writing itself.

But Sion hadn't moved.

He'd been like that for hours. Maybe longer. Time didn't count the same way in this room. And maybe that's why he'd come back here because the world outside was starting to pull at him again. And he didn't know if he wanted to go.

Downstairs, his mum was making breakfast. Toast, eggs, the good butter, the kind she only bought when she felt hopeful. His father was outside, sweeping the front path for no reason other than it gave him something to do. The house had returned to its rhythms.

But Sion hadn't. Not yet.

He reached into the tin box, fingers brushing past the feather, past the folded pieces of paper. At the bottom was a small object: a charm from his childhood. Something plastic and silly, a red dinosaur keychain with one eye scratched off. He held it in his palm for a moment, then placed it next to the map.

It looked so small. So ordinary. Like a memory that had outlived its moment.

He was tired.

Not the kind of tired that sleep could fix, but the kind that came from holding too much. Of carrying the pain of others for so long that he'd forgotten where his own ended. The voices had grown quiet recently. The monsters too. He hadn't drawn a new one in days. Not because they were gone, but because something was shifting.

Sion felt it inside him. A question, unspoken.

Stay, or go. Forget, or remember. Live in one world or in between them.

The attic began to change. Not visibly. But in feeling. The edges of the room softened. The corners turned vague. It was starting again—that thinning between moments. He could feel the pull, the way the walls breathed. If he let himself slip, even just a little, he knew he'd be back in that stream of time again—floating through the past, whispering between lives.

But if he stayed… If he let go of that pull, if he stayed fully here, then he might forget. The memories might fade. The names, the places, the creatures, all of it might soften into shadows.

He could return to being just a boy. Or he could become something else entirely. A keeper of threads. A whisper between worlds.

His hand moved to the map. Gently, his fingers touched the centre, where the boy with no face sat crosslegged. The place where all paths met.

The room gave no answer. Because it wasn't the attic's choice. It was his.

A tear rolled down his cheek, slow and quiet.

Not from sadness.

From love.

He didn't speak, but he whispered something only the room could hear.

Then he stood.

He took the map and placed it in the box, right beneath the feather. Closed the lid. Held it close.

And walked out of the attic.

Downstairs, his mum looked up from the stove. His father paused mid-sweep, brow furrowed. They didn't speak.

But something had changed.

Sion was here.

Fully here.

And yet...

Somewhere deep in the spaces between heartbeats, between ticking clocks and quiet corners—his whisper remained. Watching. Listening. Still carrying what others could not.

"I won't leave. But I won't be whole Not if it means someone else might break."   *ither.*

CHAPTER 19
The Whisper That Stayed

Years passed. Quietly, as they often do.

The house remained, though its rooms looked different now. The walls were newly painted. The fourth room with the big window had a desk where a cot used to be. The attic had been tidied but never cleared, the feather still there, the faint scent of pencil shavings lingering like old perfume. A stillness held in the floorboards, as if the house knew better than to forget.

Sion's parents never fully explained what happened. Not to the neighbours. Not even to themselves. One morning, he simply didn't come down for breakfast, and when they went up, they found his room just as he'd left it. His iPad plugged in. A sketch left unfinished. A single whispered word written in the corner of the screen: *stay*.

He was not gone. But he was no longer only here.

There were no footprints to follow. No sign of a runaway. Just an absence that didn't ache, it shimmered.

His parents searched in all the ways grieving people do. Phone calls. Hospitals. The police. But somewhere deep, they both knew this wasn't a disappearance you could trace with logic.

His mother said it felt like standing in a room after someone just left, you still smell their scent, still feel the warmth where they were sitting, even though you didn't hear the door open or close.

And then things began to happen.

Subtle things.

In Bristol, a young girl about to cross the street stopped suddenly, just before a car ran the red light.

In Swansea, an old man changed his bus route for no reason, and sat beside someone who hadn't spoken to anyone in weeks. They talked the whole way to town.

A social worker in Newport woke from a dream she couldn't quite recall, but with a clear image in her mind: a child's face. She searched through her files. Found a missed call. Called back. And stopped a tragedy.

They were all small things. Inexplicable. Quiet. But often followed by the same thought: *I don't know why I did that... it just felt right.*

And then the drawings started to appear.

A church noticeboard in Sheffield had one pinned up with no name: a sketch of a girl in a red coat, holding a folded scarf. A shopkeeper in Birmingham found one tucked between the pages of an old ledger: a boy standing beneath a tree with no leaves, but the sun shining above him. In a café in Manchester, someone left behind a page showing two people holding hands through a wall of vines, each vine cut clean.

No one knew where they came from. They were never signed. But people felt them. Deeply. Like waking from a dream and suddenly understanding something that had never made sense before.

In each drawing, there was always one familiar thread.

A figure, quiet. Small. Sometimes just an outline. Always holding a pencil.

Whispers followed.

Someone in Cardiff swore they'd seen that same boy, years ago, in a dream. A woman in her sixties remembered him from a hospital corridor in 1975, but couldn't explain how. A child claimed a boy had helped her find her dog, though the CCTV only showed the animal arriving on its own.

These weren't ghost stories. They weren't urban myths.

They were… memories.

Or perhaps echoes.

Sion hadn't spoken again. Not aloud. But his voice, his *whisper*, remained. In moments of clarity. In sudden compassion. In the split-second choices that saved a life or softened a heart.

He had chosen this long ago, when the world's pain had called to him louder than his own fear.

He became part of the stream between moments. Never staying too long. Never letting go completely.

A name spoken in silence.

A whisper that stayed.

Somewhere, in a time that wasn't quite now, a boy sat cross-legged beneath a tree that bloomed in winter. He held a pencil. Not to draw, but just to hold. To remember. To wait.

And far away, a child breathed easier. A mother forgave. A father stayed.

And the world whispered back.

EPILOGUE
The House with Quiet Walls

The house still stands.

People walk past it now without noticing. A simple terrace, paint fading a little on the edges. The curtains always drawn just enough to let the light in. To strangers, it's nothing remarkable. Just another home on a quiet street near the brook.

But the house remembers.

The floors remember soft footsteps at odd hours. The fourth room still reflects more than it should in the window glass. And the attic, though mostly empty, has an air about it. The kind that makes you pause before switching off the light. Not fearful. Just… aware.

His mother still lives there. Her hair is more silver than black now. Her steps slower. But her eyes are softer than they've ever been. She doesn't look for him anymore, not in the world outside. But sometimes she pauses mid-step, as if listening. And she smiles, just faintly, like someone who hears a song others can't.

She keeps a box beneath her bed.

Inside it: folded drawings. Notes she can't bring herself to throw away. One worn jumper with sleeves too long. And a feather, black, curved at the tip, still strange in its silence.

Every now and then, she opens the box.

Not to grieve.

But to remember the boy who carried other people's pain so they didn't have to.

The boy who didn't speak, but was never silent.

The boy who whispered once.

And was still heard.

CLOSING REMARKS

For Those Who Carry Too Much

If you've ever sat in the dark and felt the weight of the world press against your chest.

If you've ever been the one who stays up, who watches, who listens too deeply and feels too much.

If you've ever been misunderstood, labelled, silenced, or told you were too quiet, too odd, too much.

Then maybe, in some way, this story is also yours.

Sion's journey was never just about gifts or powers. It was about *burden*. About the strange and sacred cost of empathy. About the quiet heroes no one sees, the ones who carry pain without needing applause, who draw light from sorrow, who listen when no one speaks.

There are many like him.

Maybe you are one.

Maybe someone you love is.

And maybe, just maybe, the next time you feel something shift, an ache eased, a fear softened, a kindness rising in your chest for no clear reason, you'll remember:

Somewhere, someone whispered for you.

And it stayed.

AUTHOR'S NOTES

This book began as a whisper.

A quiet thought during one of those nights when the world felt too loud and too fast, and I wondered, what happens to the children who don't fit inside the boxes we build for them? What happens to those who speak in their own ways, feel more than they know how to say, and carry the weight of things they can't explain?

Sion came to me slowly. Not with fireworks or fanfare, but with a hush. He arrived like a boy who had been waiting to be noticed. He didn't ask to be understood, only to be seen.

This is a work of fiction. But those who know me and know my family, may recognise something more. You'll sense the thread that runs beneath every chapter. You'll know this story is inspired by our own experiences, our quiet struggles, and our deep love for our son, **Shann**.

Much of what Sion carries, Shann has carried too. Not with powers or time-slipping journeys, but with courage, silence, creativity, and a heart that feels far more than it lets on.

This story is for the ones who are rarely at the centre of the room, but who still hold everything together. For those whose silence isn't emptiness, but depth. For every child who's been called difficult, or strange, or too sensitive—for every adult who remembers being that child. For the parents who keep showing up, even in exhaustion and confusion and fear. For the teachers who look past behaviours and see hearts.

And for anyone who's ever wished they could take away someone else's pain, this is a quiet reminder that sometimes, love is already doing that, in ways you don't even realise.

Sion's powers are not just fantasy. They are reflections of very real things: the ache of empathy, the beauty of creative expression, and the unseen ways some people absorb the world's hurt to give it back healed.

Thank you for listening to his story.

And if it's helped you whisper a little more kindly to your own pain, or someone else's, then that, I believe, is enough.

WHISPERS ON PAPER

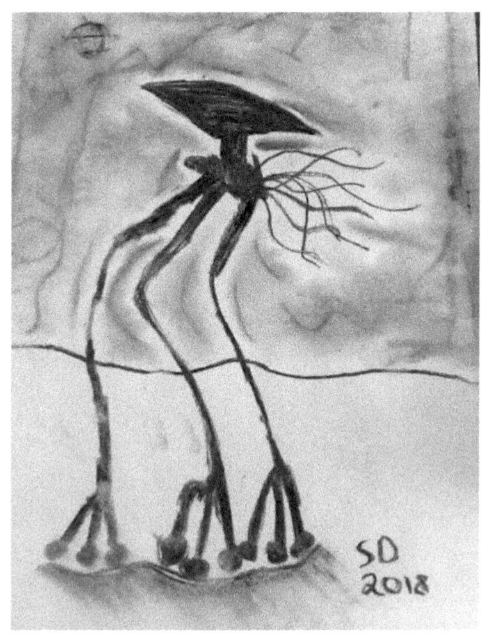

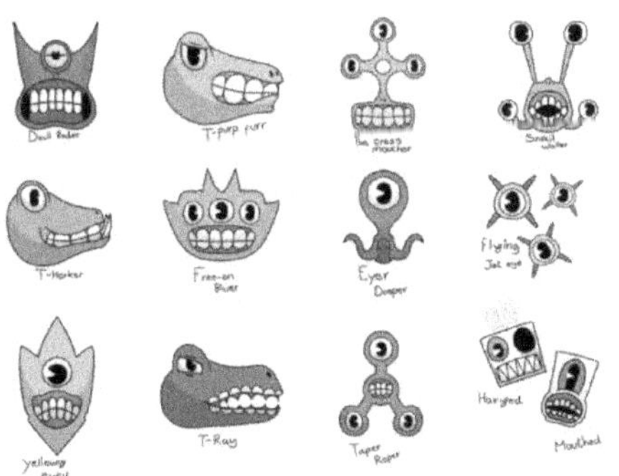

ciTy LIE

Published in Collaboration with Noble
Legacy Publishing

www.noblelegacypublishing.co.uk

www.ingramcontent.com/pod-product-compliance
Lightning Source LLC
Chambersburg PA
CBHW040229170726
48295CB00014B/859